"I have a big problem," Aaron said, his voice full of gravel. **"I'm not looking for a relationship."**

"Neither am I," Stella interrupted then gripped his wrist, keeping his warm palm pressed to her face. She knew what she wanted and what she didn't want. She didn't want a relationship, or to be hurt. And she sure as hell didn't want to lose his touch.

His pupils flared, the black swallowing the blue of his irises. "I can't help wanting you. Wanting to kiss you again. Wanting more." His thumb swiped her bottom lip in provocation.

She sighed, closed her eyes, enjoyed the moment that felt like that weightless feeling at the top of a swing.

She opened her eyes. "I want you too, but I'm not sure that it's wise." The last few words came out a whisper, totally lacking conviction.

But seriously, who cared about wisdom with chemistry this good? She'd be leaving as soon as her transfer came through. Surely she could indulge in her ultimate fantasy: one night with Aaron Bennett.

Question was, would she survive it?

Dear Reader,

Having lived in a small English village for many years, I found it enchanting to write Aaron and Stella's story in such an idyllic setting. Compared to that of the city, there is a different dynamic to the close-knit communities of rural life as shown by the medical scenarios I threw my hero and heroine into. By pushing London-loving Stella out of her comfort zone, it becomes clear that her roots are an undeniable part of her identity. I know this firsthand being born and raised in Wales and now living in New Zealand! This was also my first story with a single parent, and I loved writing the scenes featuring Charlie. Showing Aaron's character through his relationship with his son really helped me to get into my hero's head and unearth different aspirational aspects of his personality.

I hope you enjoy *How to Resist the Single Dad*.

Love

JC x

HOW TO RESIST THE SINGLE DAD

———

JC HARROWAY

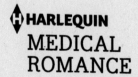

HARLEQUIN

MEDICAL
ROMANCE

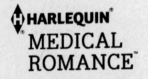

HARLEQUIN®
MEDICAL ROMANCE™

Recycling programs for this product may not exist in your area.

ISBN-13: 978-1-335-73743-4

How to Resist the Single Dad

Harlequin Enterprises ULC
22 Adelaide St. West, 41st Floor
Toronto, Ontario M5H 4E3, Canada
www.Harlequin.com

Printed in U.S.A.

Lifelong romance addict **JC Harroway** took a break from her career as a junior doctor to raise a family and found her calling as a Harlequin author instead. She now lives in New Zealand and finds that writing feeds her very real obsession with happy endings and the endorphin rush they create. You can follow her at jcharroway.com, and on Facebook, Twitter and Instagram.

Books by JC Harroway

Harlequin Medical Romance

Forbidden Fling with Dr. Right

Harlequin Dare

One Night Only
Forbidden to Taste
Forbidden to Touch
The Proposition
Bad Business
Bad Reputation
Bad Mistake
Bound to You
Tempting the Enemy

Visit the Author Profile page
at Harlequin.com for more titles.

To Becky, my horse-loving, Wellie-wearing,
Land Rover–driving friend.

CHAPTER ONE

Watching Dr Aaron Bennett speak from the main lecture-theatre podium of London's City Hospital gave Stella Wright serious crush flashbacks. Of course she had fancied him. Who wouldn't? But, where her ridiculous teenage obsession had been abstract, that of the shy four-teen-year-old she'd once been, now she struggled to focus on his lecture to this year's intake of general-practitioner trainees.

Like an expensive single-malt whisky, Aaron had only improved with age. He sported a head of sandy blond hair that had the tendency to flop over his aristocratic brow. His dark-framed glasses made his bright blue eyes—ones she had once considered *dreamy*—appear more intense. He wore a fine-knit V-necked jumper over his shirt, and when he had turned his back on his audience to point at the screen, Stella had almost drooled at his toned backside. In fact, his entire look brought to mind a sexy professor fantasy that Stella should in no way indulge.

She dragged her eyes away. She was long ago done with charmers and Aaron Bennett epitomised the definition. Or at least he had during his twenties and early thirties in their Cotswold village of Abbotsford.

With a reputation as a charismatic playboy, he'd regularly blasted back into their sleepy village for a weekend of hedonistic fun, always driving a fast sports car and bringing with him a gaggle of friends looking for a wild party at the country estate his parents still ran. His notorious reputation had been the talk of the town, every eligible woman and mother alike wondering when the local heartthrob would settle down. Return home for good and take up his place in the small community.

To everyone's surprise, he eventually had.

And now, here in London—Stella's home these past nine years—he seemed somehow out of place, even though he himself had trained and worked in the capital.

Of course, she hadn't heard a word of what he'd actually said for the last five minutes since she'd first drifted off into a lust-filled daydream and then been reminded of another Cotswolds smooth-talker, one who'd done such a good job of breaking her heart, she'd sworn off relationships at the tender age of eighteen. Which was why, when he closed his laptop at the end of his lecture and said her name, Stella almost slid from her seat to disappear beneath the desk.

'Could Stella Wright please see me? Thank you.' He swept his gaze over the doctors filling the auditorium.

In case her friends were watching and wondering what she had done to upset the teacher, Stella forced her face to freeze on a benign smile, while her insides tumbled over themselves to make sense of his request. What could Aaron Bennett want with *her*? Yes, they came from the same small village, where his family descended from a long line of landed gentry. She knew all about his tragic past, which like Stella's own notoriety had no doubt been prime village-gossip fodder. But they'd never actually spoken to one another.

Fourteen- or fifteen-year-old Stella would have swooned.

It was a good thing that twenty-seven-year-old committed singleton Dr Stella Wright's swooning days were over.

As Aaron fell into conversation with one of the keener registrars, a gorgeous blonde Stella knew well enough to guess had approached him with an intelligent question that had nothing to do with his backside or dreamy eyes, Stella headed for the stairs and raked her scattered wits for something to say other than *Hi, I used to have a crush on you.*

For goodness' sake, he was one of her educational supervisors. Her past and irrelevant infatuation with Dr Delicious should serve only to remind her of the momentous reasons she'd left Abbotsford for the big-city lights of London in the first place. Why she'd followed in her sister Darcy's footsteps and moved here, reinventing herself in the process.

Heartbreak Harry, as she'd named her ex.

Stella cast a glance at Aaron. Had he remembered her from Abbotsford, heard the gossip?

Still in conversation with the blonde, he seemed completely oblivious to Stella. Perhaps he didn't know she existed. Well, that suited her just fine.

She paused halfway down the steps to reply to a group text from her GP trainee friends, who were about to scatter across the country for the final eighteen months of their training.

Clubbing tonight—last night before we all disperse.

Stella smiled, a spasm of nostalgia pinching her ribs. She was staying in London. She loved living here. The vibrancy, the constant bustle, the anonymity of being one person out of millions. But she would miss her crew. Who would go clubbing with her now? Her sister was recently all loved up, so she had no hope of dragging Darcy out on the town.

Just then her friend Tom called out from the front of the lecture theatre, where there was a bottleneck at the exit.

'Stells.' He waved, snagging her attention away from Aaron's broad shoulders. 'Pre-drinks at the pub tonight? Wear your dancing shoes.' Tom offered a playful wink, a shimmy to a tune only he could hear and left the lecture theatre.

Tom didn't do subtle. There was no way Aaron had missed their interaction.

Prickles danced over her skin, a sensation of Aaron's observation that should have been uncomfortable but instead left her wondering if he was still single or remained unattached after the death of his wife.

She looked up, sucking in a breath as her stare collided directly with his. He had been watching her, his conversation seemingly abandoned as he stared intently.

A small smile twitched her cheeks while she battled the incendiary effects of that direct eye contact. It could have only lasted a second or two, but it was long enough for Stella's pulse to skyrocket and her breath to trap under her diaphragm as if she had a stitch.

Had she imagined a tightening of his facial muscles between his brows, the thinning of his lips? Was he judging her penchant for having a good time, letting down her hair, dancing?

Clearly they had little in common beyond coming from the same village.

Stella lingered over the last few steps to the front of the auditorium, waiting for him to wind up his conversation.

The other doctor headed for the exit, leaving her and Aaron alone. The vast theatre, which could easily seat three hundred people, shrank to the size of a broom cupboard. The closer she stepped, the more attractive he became. Nerves accosted her stomach at his tall, imposing masculinity. Their differences—the age gap and the country-boy, city-girl chasm—seemed increasingly trivial.

'Dr Wright, thanks for waiting behind,' he said, his deep voice confident and full of warmth. He tossed his glasses onto the podium and held out his hand.

'No problem,' she croaked, shaking his hand firmly in order to boost her wobbling confidence. Alone with her and up close he seemed to have morphed into the hottest man she'd ever met.

With his glasses removed, his bold blue eyes

were more vibrant. His biceps and pecs were clearly demarcated beneath his jumper. His tie was ever so slightly askew, lending him a roguish, devil-may-care vibe that tied all of his attractive qualities together with a bright red bow, a combination that packed a considerable punch to Stella's poor neglected libido.

She swallowed. Time to get a grip. His hotness was completely irrelevant.

a) He had looked disapproving at her clubbing plans.

b) Despite no trace of a dad bod, Stella knew from her parents that he had a young son.

c) Perhaps the most important factor of all: Stella hadn't dated since Harry.

'I won't keep you long.' He dropped her hand.

Stella wiped her palm on her trouser leg as discreetly as possible, praying like crazy that he hadn't felt the judders zapping along her nerves as they touched. This close she could smell his aftershave, which was woodsy and fresh and made her homesick for autumn walks through the countryside and roaring fires on a cold day.

'What's this about?' she said, the flash of what looked like guilt or sympathy on his face raising her defensive hackles. Was he recalling what he knew of her from the small talk that had once circulated in Abbotsford?

She felt like a germ swimming in a petri dish.

Privacy was scarce in village life, and Stella had left the Cotswolds for university under a cloud of unjust gossip that still had the ability to make her shudder with shame. Not because the rumours had been true—beyond being young and naive and falling head over heels for the wrong man with a young son and a complicated past he'd lied about, she'd done nothing wrong. But because she couldn't for the life of herself fathom that she'd once been so gullible, so lovestruck, so pitiable.

If only she could forget the humiliation of not only having her tender teenaged heart broken for the first time, but also being unfairly vilified as some sort of Lolita-esque home-wrecker...

'I'm afraid there's an issue with your GP placement,' Aaron said without reference to Abbotsford. Perhaps he didn't recognise her after all.

Stella winced at the bedside manner of his tone. 'What issue?'

Aaron's stare roamed her face as if peeling away her layers of armour, one by one. Did he have to look at her with such...intimacy?

'I'm afraid your assigned GP, Dr Roberts at Ealing Health has suffered a serious medical emergency and will no longer be able to accommodate you at his surgery.'

Stella covered her mouth in shock. 'Is he okay?' *Poor Dr Roberts.*

'He suffered a myocardial infarction yesterday,' Aaron said, 'and underwent coronary artery stenting this morning, but obviously he isn't expected back at work for some time.'

Stella nodded, realisation dawning. She was due to start her GP placement at Ealing Health on Monday. Dr Roberts was meant to supervise her training for the next year and a half.

'So what happens now?' she asked, her skin tight with prickles. 'Presumably I'll be placed at my second-choice surgery in Hammersmith.'

'I'm afraid not.' Aaron's lips flattened, drawing Stella's gaze reluctantly from his piercing and perceptive eyes. Idly she wondered if he'd be a good kisser. He must be to have earned his reputation.

He cleared his throat, drawing Stella back to the conversation. 'They already have a GP trainee there.'

'So where exactly will I be placed?' Stella's blood started to roar in her ears. She empathised with poor Dr Roberts, she truly did, but there had to be a suitable alternative. The powers that be at the Royal College of General Practitioners must have a plan B for this kind of unfortunate eventuality.

Aaron frowned, his lips twisted with frustration, a move that did nothing to diminish his rugged good looks. 'As most of the placements have already been finalised, you've been assigned to my practice in the Cotswolds.'

Stella's mouth fell open. 'What...? But...' No. Abbotsford was a part of her previous life, a life she'd abandoned when she'd wrapped up her tattered heart, left behind tragic small-town Stella and moved permanently to London. She had abandoned the misty-eyed and gauche teenager she had been, grown up, reinvented herself. Here she was fun and free Stella with a career she adored, a buzzing social life and an enviable shoe collection to complement her party outfits.

Aaron rubbed his hand along his cleanly shaven jaw as if he was as irritated with the arrangement as she was, which inflamed her further.

'I'll go anywhere else,' she pleaded. 'There must be somewhere else.' She was being rude, but his news couldn't be any less welcome.

'I'm afraid not.' His polite smile was tight. 'But bear in mind that I didn't ask for a trainee either.'

She flushed and then qualified, 'What I mean is that I specifically requested to be assigned to a London practice. I'm more likely to receive a broad experience in the city and this is where I plan on living and working. I've no interest in a village practice.'

She had left village life behind.

At her unintentional put-down, the corners of Aaron's eyes crinkled, his irises chilling two shades icier.

He crossed his arms over that broad chest and this time her keen eyes caught a glimpse of golden chest hair behind the loosened collar of his shirt. 'That may be the case, but there is nowhere else at such short notice.' Now his expression sported as much frustration as Stella felt coiling in her stomach.

Her heart sank, the bad news in no way softened by the flare of lust running through her veins.

No, no, no. She couldn't work for her ancient crush, and she couldn't spend the next year and a half living in the village that featured at the centre of her most shameful regret.

Perfect.

Aaron's lush lips moved. Instead of imagined kisses, Stella listened as he confirmed her worst fears. 'I'm afraid, Dr Wright, that, like it or not, we're stuck with each other.'

CHAPTER TWO

AARON STAMPED HIS feet in order to drive some blood into his frigid toes and pressed the phone closer to his ear to hear over the chatter of some rowdy passers-by. The streets around City Hospital were conveniently littered with long-established aptly named pubs: The Surgeon's Arms, Nightingale Inn, and his personal favourite: The Crown and Canker. It was Friday night. Spirits were high.

'Okay, Charlie. Dad will help you build a castle in the morning, I promise,' he said to his five-year-old.

'Will you be here before breakfast, Daddy?'

'Of course I will. I promise.' He winced. A slither of that special brand of guilt reserved only for parents snaked down his spine. 'Does Grandma have our favourite cereal, the one that makes our muscles strong and our brains smart like a superhero?'

His son's boyish chuckle warmed him through,

as it never failed to do. If only it could permanently drive away the constant fear that he was making a hash of raising his son solo.

'Yes, Daddy. See you at breakfast. Goodnight. I love you.'

'I love you too, Champ.'

Aaron spoke briefly to his mother, confirming that he'd be back in Abbotsford first thing in the morning and then hung up the phone. For a handful of seconds he stared at the blank screen, paralysed by familiar remorse. He tried to minimise his nights away from Charlie. He'd made a promise to his tiny days-old son that he'd always be there for him, be both parents rolled into one, so that the boy would never want for anything. The only reason he'd taken the GP lecturing position at City Hospital was because he could make a difference, give something back to the general-practitioner training programme and limit his absence from home to one night a month.

It was silly, but to Aaron the time away seemed interminable.

He slipped his phone into his pocket, struggling with the sense of failure and regret that became heightened whenever they were apart. But no amount of self-flagellation changed their circumstances.

It was still just the two of them. The Boys' Club. Snapping from his trance, Aaron ducked out of the dreary mid-November weather and inside the warmth of The Crown and Canker. The sweet smell of real ale and wood smoke accosted his nostrils and provided a sense of nostalgia akin to a comforting embrace. He cherished every moment of being a single dad, but after a long week at work, he couldn't deny himself his one vice: a pint or two of good beer in good company.

And tonight, more than ever, he wished to forget the new distraction in his life, one he certainly didn't need: Stella Wright.

He'd instantly spotted her familiar name on his list of GP trainees. The first time he'd seen her at City Hospital, back in the summer, when he'd attended his interview, he'd recognised her, despite only previously knowing her from afar. She was the kind of woman you noticed. Strikingly attractive, her kaleidoscopic green-brown eyes bright with intelligence and that ready, infectious laugh that had seemed to demand his attention. Just like today, she'd been with the tall redheaded man who'd beckoned her from the front of the lecture theatre. Was she out with him now, laughing, drinking, dancing? Clearly they were a well-matched couple.

No wonder she despised the idea of leaving London.

Sleepy Abbotsford and a hick GP like him

had little to offer a young, vibrant socialite like Stella Wright.

I'll go anywhere else.

Oh, her plea had kneed him right in the groin, because he harboured similar reluctance. The last thing he wanted was an unwilling trainee messing with his ordered existence. He had vowed, after losing his wife, Molly, only days after she'd given birth to their only child, that providing Charlie with stability and more love than he could ever need would be Aaron's number-one priority.

He sighed. There would be no avoiding the issue when she arrived in his GP practice on Monday morning. He'd have a major complication to manage, one with mesmerising hazel eyes, a captivating smile and a stimulating personality. One who unconsciously reminded him that he was more than a rural GP, a father, a son. He was also a man, a part of himself he'd sidelined for the past five years.

Fortunately for him, not only did Stella likely have a boyfriend, but Aaron had also become a pro at multitasking since Charlie's birth. If he focused on his priorities—Charlie and his work—he could keep any attraction he felt towards Stella the way it should be: irrelevant.

Dodging a raucous crowd who appeared fully committed to celebrating the start of the weekend, Aaron scanned the crowded pub. He spotted his old friend, Joe Austin and Joe's girl-friend, Darcy—who just happened to be Stella's sister—in a nook near one of the windows. Aaron waved, stretching above a sea of heads and weaved through the Friday night revellers, his spirits rising in the buoyant atmosphere.

This was exactly what he needed tonight. Forget Stella Wright.

He arrived at Joe and Darcy's table, his stomach swooping to his boots. Stella sat with them. He hadn't spied her from across the pub. Now his blood surged with adrenaline, both thrilling and dreaded.

Their eyes clashed like a high-speed collision. Hers were defiant, challenging in a way that heated his blood.

'You made it,' said Joe, grinning in welcome and rising to his feet.

'Yeah, sorry I'm late.' Aaron dragged his stare away from Stella, whose lips had flattened with disapproval the minute he joined them, and greeted Darcy. 'Lovely to see you again.' He kissed Darcy's cheek.

'You remember my sister from Abbotsford, of course,' said Darcy, seemingly unaware of the frosty atmosphere surrounding him and her sister.

Aaron shrugged out of his coat. 'A little, yes.'

He offered Stella a nod of recognition and a tight smile that he hoped concealed the rush of turmoil her presence created.

Of course their age difference, he at least fourteen years her senior, meant he hadn't been familiar with Stella when they'd both lived in Abbotsford beyond knowing that she existed. He had vague memories of Darcy's younger half-siblings, of there being three Wright sisters, but then he had left home for university, become too absorbed in his own life and only returned to the village to live six years ago.

'But we met properly earlier today.' He cast another glance at Stella, finding her mouth pursed with displeasure in a way that told Aaron she hadn't been aware that he was invited this evening.

'Oh,' Darcy chuckled, glancing at Stella with mischief in her eyes. 'Did you know that she had an enormous teenage crush on you back in the day? Hanging on every word of the gossip from your famous weekend parties.'

'Oh, please.' Stella dismissed her sister with an eye roll, her expression feigning boredom. Only the flush colouring her high cheekbones gave away any discomfort.

'Is that right?' he said, disregarding the increased thrill of his pulse and the renewed rumbling of fascination this news provoked. He placed his coat on the window seat lining the ancient bay window, a spot that would position him directly opposite Stella, and smiled benignly at the woman who had all but told him earlier that his small country practice was lame.

She had certainly outgrown any interest in him.

He dragged in a strengthening breath like the ones that he had employed to help him ignore her presence in his lecture. Until her supervisor's ill-health had forced Aaron's hand, forced him to speak with her directly. Forced him to invite her to his quiet country practice where he reigned, controller of his predictably stable universe. And Charlie's.

Stella tossed her dark hair over one shoulder and turned her apathetic gaze his way. 'I didn't know you were joining us tonight…that is, joining *them.*' She pointed to her sister and Joe, who watched their stilted interaction with barely concealed amusement.

What was it about her that drew his curiosity? So she was the first woman in years to ignite a spark in his libido. That meant nothing. Even if she wasn't with the guy he'd seen her with on more than one occasion, he had his life just the way he wanted it and he wouldn't risk disruption to the status quo for something as trivial as sexual attraction. Especially not for a woman who would not only be his trainee, but who also thought his life, his practice, probably even he himself were dull and provincial.

Aaron shrugged. 'Is it a problem?' He had come here to relax, to catch up with Joe. He refused to spend the night trading gibes with Stella, even if it was the most exhilaration he'd had in ages.

She shook her head. 'I'm not staying.' As if to prove her point, she stood, scraping back her chair on the ancient floorboards. 'I'm here with people. We're going clubbing later.' She tilted her chin as if expecting some comment.

He didn't need her reminder to know that she likely viewed everything about him with derision, or that in addition to their age difference, their personalities, their interests couldn't be more different.

He hid his sigh of relief, grateful that she would soon be leaving. She looked far too sexy in her little black dress, and he wasn't used to noticing members of the opposite sex. But there was no ignoring Stella. He looked down to where her long, slender legs ended in a pair of gravity-defying heels—clearly he was a weaker man than he would have thought.

'I see you're wearing your dancing shoes.' He couldn't help but badger her, if only to keep her at a distance.

Stella nodded, defiance pursing her lush lips. 'Yes.' She gave his outfit—jeans, a navy sweater and boots—a return once-over that made his body temperature rise a few degrees.

'You're welcome to join us, if you like.' Amusement sparkled in her eyes. 'Although Darcy and Joe have declined. Fuddy-duddies.'

It was issued as a challenge, one he was only too happy to decline as Joe and Darcy merely sniggered. 'No, thanks. My clubbing days are over. But enjoy yourself. As you probably recall, there aren't any nightclubs in Abbotsford, so it's sensible to get your fix before Monday.'

Mock horror widened her eyes. 'How will I ever endure such a sleepy backwater?'

He grinned. 'Oh, we find a way to make our own fun.' Aaron looked away from the tantalising sparks of fire, for which he liked to think he could take credit. For a man who avoided complications, who relished the quiet, predictable life, he was having way too much fun sparring with this woman.

'Unfortunately for her,' he said to Joe and Darcy in explanation, 'Stella will be joining me as my trainee at the practice from next week.'

At his reminder that she'd been far from enthusiastic earlier, Stella opened her mouth as if to speak and then closed it again, her eyes narrowing.

He took advantage of her temporary speechlessness. 'Well, it looks like it's my round. Can I get anyone a drink?' With Joe and Darcy's order fresh in his mind—Stella had declined—he made his way to the bar, putting some much-needed space between them.

He'd just about reached the front of the queue when someone jostled him from behind. Aaron glanced over his shoulder at the same moment someone grabbed his arm.

'Oh, sorry.' A red-faced Stella braced her hand on his bicep while she corrected her balance. She looked none too pleased that she'd been forced to touch him rather than wobble from her heels.

Aaron took advantage of the fortuitous split second and inhaled the delicious scent of her perfume, enjoying the heat of her body so close and the blush staining her cheeks.

'Did you change your mind about the drink?' Aaron asked, glancing down to where her hand still rested on his arm. He dared not think about how long it had been since a woman had touched him; he was already ancient and out of touch in this woman's eyes.

Stella snatched her hand away. 'No, I didn't. I just came over to clarify a few things with you.'

Ah, she'd come with an agenda. Why bother if she found him so…objectionable? Perhaps he made her nervous. She certainly seemed a little jittery, her eyes darting around the pub as if seeking out an escape route.

'Oh?' He stared into those amazingly spangled eyes, feeling a little like the man he'd been at Stella's age—single but never short of the company of a beautiful and fun woman, confident that he was master of his own destiny, cramming pleasure into every second of his free time. Awareness of her warmth still invading his personal space, of the way her dress clung to her breasts and of the way she made him feel twice as alive as he'd been before she appeared in his consciousness, forced him to redirect his stare to the selection of spirit bottles behind the bar.

Off-limits, way off-limits.

She was too young for him. She would be working for him, no matter how much they both begrudged that twist of fate. And, as always, Charlie needed all of Aaron's spare energy.

'The concerns I voiced about my placement have nothing to do with you personally,' she said, a soft aggrieved huff passing her full lips. 'I hardly know you.'

Said lips were slicked with some sort of shiny gloss. Aaron couldn't help but wonder how it would taste. He needed to focus on her grievances, not indulge inappropriate fantasies.

'It's nothing to do with your practice specifically,' she continued as she did her best to keep her body as far away from his as possible in the crowded bar, a feat that involved shifting her weight from one foot to the other in time with the flow of bodies around them.

'It's not even about the lack of dancing facilities.' Her mouth twitched as she held his stare.

He dragged his eyes away from the temptation of those lips, delighted to discover her sense of humour. It only increased her attractiveness.

She sobered then. 'I had a plan. A plan that doesn't include returning to Abbotsford.'

Aaron nodded in sympathy, his mind abuzz. So it was the place that offended her, not him. But that made no sense. Her parents still lived in the village. She'd grown up there. Would it be so terrible to spend time in a place so familiar? Now he wished that he had paid more attention whenever he heard mention of the Wright family over the years. Maybe then he would understand her reluctance.

Perhaps it was related to the man he had seen her with.

He swallowed the foreign taste of jealousy, his gaze flicking to the very guy, whom Aaron had spotted in conversation with a group of late twenty-somethings at the other end of the bar.

'It's just that when you've been expecting one thing and looking forward to the next stage of your career…' she shrugged '…and then it's suddenly snatched away…'

He wasn't unfeeling. He could understand that she wanted to be close to the man if they were an item. He himself had trained in London and never imagined that he would return to Abbotsford so soon, until he'd met and fallen in love with local woman Molly.

His life had been perfect for a while. Until he'd messed it up.

'Yes,' he said, his throat raw with guilt, 'life is great for disrupting best-laid plans.' No one knew that better than him. Healthy women weren't supposed to die after giving birth to healthy babies in modern, first-world hospitals.

'Anyway,' continued Stella, 'as you pointed out, you are just as stuck with me as I am with you.'

She stared as if expecting him to wave a magic wand and reassign her to another practice. If he could do that he would have done it before even telling her of the change in placement. With his commitments to the educational-supervisor role and to his personal life, he had no desire to foster a reluctant and disappointed trainee who pushed his buttons and left him…restless.

Aaron winced. 'Yes. I apologise for the way that sounded. What I meant was that with my lecturing timetable, I had no intention of taking on a registrar this year. Although, as you yourself insinuated, my quaint country practice likely has little to teach you, anyway.'

He should stop goading her, otherwise Monday would be unbearable. They were polar opposites personality-wise, and she would clearly struggle to respect his professional opinion. It was doomed to complication, something he avoided at all costs. He'd had enough of that in his life, and he owed it to Charlie, and to Molly, to make their son's upbringing as normal and drama-free as possible.

So what the hell was he doing?

Stella narrowed her eyes as if he'd insulted her rather than voiced the facts. 'You know, until we met this afternoon, I believed the hype about you, your reputation as one of the Cotswolds' nicest and best GPs.' She fisted a hand on her hip.

'Thank you,' he deadpanned. A wave of heat and shame flooded Aaron's body. There was something about this woman that made him uncharacteristically adversarial. To make amends, first thing tomorrow, he would appeal to the powers that be to find Stella a more mutually acceptable placement.

'Look.' He adjusted his tone in surrender. 'I can understand that you don't want to be so far away from your boyfriend.' Aaron tilted his head in the guy's direction. 'Let me see what I can arrange, okay? If you really hate the idea of a rural practice in Abbotsford, I'll apply to the college to have you reassigned as soon as possible. It's not our intention to make your GP training torture, after all.' He managed his most cordial smile, dismissing the way she seemed to have awoken him as irrelevant.

'Tom's not my boyfriend.' Stella frowned.

Aaron's heartrate soared, as if one obstacle had been removed. But there were plenty more; best he remember that.

'He's just a friend,' she said, lifting her chin. 'I'm single and my preferring to stay in London has nothing to do with a man, I assure you.'

Except her emphasis, her dismissal made it sound exactly that. The knowledge he was free to find her as attractive as he liked inflamed him. This was bad, bad news. She was hard enough to ignore when he had designated her neatly out of bounds, but now that he knew they were both single, his imagination was free to wander. Right down Lust Street.

Nope, not going there. But a little harmless sparring could surely be returned to the table. He couldn't have her thinking him dull as dishwater.

'Don't be too emphatic,' he joked, his lips twitching with mischief. 'Or you'll have me wondering if your reluctance to work for me is from fear that your ancient crush will resurface.'

He needed to stop this inappropriate informality, but it had been so long since he'd even noticed members of the opposite sex, let alone wanted to talk—no, spar—with one. And he would need to employ humour and every defence known to man in order to keep her at arm's length once they were working side by side.

'I would never change my life for a relationship.' She huffed, unimpressed in a way that made him desperate to shock her and watch her reaction.

'And as for my ancient crush,' she swept her stare from his eyes to his toes and back, 'you shouldn't put too much store in what my sister says. Fifteen-year-old me was also madly in love with every member of the boy band of the moment and several cartoon characters, so don't take it too personally.'

Aaron chuckled. *Touché.*

Then she upped the ante, leaned close as if about to impart a secret. Aaron's body reacted to her proximity as if his libido was responding to a flashing green light. If it wasn't for Charlie and the fact that he'd had his chance at happiness and messed up, big time, he'd would have been seriously afraid for the week ahead.

Stella's breath tickled his neck. 'See you Monday, boss,' she whispered and sauntered off, leaving him confused, conflicted and neck deep in the delusion of possibility.

He abandoned the view of her retreat, the inevitable sinking feeling putting things back into perspective. This round, he would concede her the final word, because he and Stella could never be anything more than a fantasy.

CHAPTER THREE

MONDAY MORNING PUT paid to a weekend of repeatedly chiding herself for getting carried away and bicker-flirting with Aaron in the pub on Friday night. As penance, Stella had donned her most professional demeanour along with her thick tights, tweed skirt and cashmere jumper. She needed the armour if she was to survive working for Aaron, and, far from the sleepy rural practice she had imagined, Abbotsford Medical Centre was a busy place.

Much to Stella's disappointment, from the moment she had walked through the door, Aaron had been polite, formal and utterly appropriate in return.

No more hot looks she wasn't sure that she'd imagined but that made her flustered. No more flirtatious banter back and forth. And his gaze never once dropped below eye level, so her comfortable but flattering outfit was utterly wasted.

She sighed, watching him talk to their latest patient, a six-year-old girl named Gabby.

She had discovered that he was one of two partners at the practice, which served Abbotsford and a clutch of surrounding villages. The building itself had been refurbished since Stella had been a patient, and there was a practice nurse, a team of receptionists and two health visitors. Stella had spent the morning sitting in on his first surgery of the day, and this afternoon she would join Aaron's minor-surgery clinic.

So far, she had been pleasantly surprised by the variety of cases she'd seen. They'd referred a young woman with Wolff-Parkinson-White Syndrome to the specialist at Gloucester General Hospital for an ablation procedure, admitted an elderly farmer with an infectious flare-up of his chronic obstructive pulmonary disease and confirmed three pregnancies. Gabby was their last patient for the morning.

'Gabby, this is Dr Wright,' he said, drawing Stella into the consultation. 'She's going to have a look at your sore throat, okay?' Gabby nodded, big, tearful eyes wary.

Ignoring Aaron's imposing presence just behind her, her body's memories of his strong muscles under her hand and the warm, delicious scent of him in the pub when she'd stumbled at the crowded bar, Stella stooped to Gabby's level where the girl sat on her concerned mother's knee.

'Can I gently feel your neck and then shine a light inside your mouth?' she asked, smiling and showing Gabby the princess and dinosaur stickers stuck to her torch.

Gabby nodded and Stella checked her neck for lymphadenopathy, carefully palpating the swollen lymph nodes on both sides.

'Open wide,' she said, taking a quick look at the girl's very inflamed throat.

'So what's your differential diagnosis?' Aaron asked Stella, smiling reassurance at the girl. 'Don't worry, I'm just quizzing Dr Wright, but you are going to feel better soon.' His attention returned to the computer monitor, his hands clacking at the keyboard keys in a totally sexy way. Was it even possible to type sexily?

Aaron did.

Stella washed her hands at the sink in the corner as she reeled off her answer. 'Viral pharyngitis, Group A streptococcal infection, scarlet fever, acute rheumatic fever and infectious mononucleosis.' She shot mother and daughter a sympathetic smile, knowing that it was likely neither of them had had much sleep the night before. 'As Gabby is pyrexial with swollen and purulent tonsils and cervical lymphadenopathy, I favour streptococcus in this case.'

'Excellent,' said Aaron, his impressed smile doing silly things to her pulse. 'Gabby, Dr Wright and I are going to give you some medicine to take, which will hopefully make you feel much better. In the meantime...' he addressed the mother '...keep her fluid intake up—ice lollies work wonders—and she needs plenty of cuddles and rest.'

He glanced at Gabby. 'Would you like me to prescribe cartoons, too?'

The girl managed a nod and a shy smile and Stella joined in, a small sigh trapped in her lungs. Aaron in GP mode would lift anyone's spirits. Even she felt better in his presence and she wasn't even sick. He showed just the right blend of compassion, confidence and explanation. She could tell from his interactions with this morning's patients that he was well respected, trusted, even treasured around these parts.

It would be easier for Stella if he matched her previous impressions. Playboy Aaron she could dismiss, no matter how attractive charismatic and charming. Except he was no longer the dashing young Romeo, haring around the village in his MG convertible, a pretty date at his side.

To stop herself from drooling over Aaron dressed in crisp chinos, a checked shirt and a soft-looking blue sweater she wanted to rub her-

self all over, Stella recalled his elderly prede-
cessor from her own childhood, Dr Millar. He'd
been cut from the same cloth as Aaron, always
bearing a warm smile that never failed to make
her feel instantly reassured, a silly dad joke and
a sympathetic ear.

But just as Aaron seemed to have changed, the
Stella who had once lived, once belonged in Abbotsford had been different—trusting and hopeful on the cusp of adulthood. And then Harry had
taken her heart, promising to take tender care of
it for ever, before stomping all over the vulnerable organ and inviting the entire village to wit-
ness his handiwork. She'd gone from belonging
to both him and to Abbotsford to being adrift in
one fell swoop.

In the nine years she had lived in London, it
had been easier to stay away and pretend that she
didn't care than to return home for the weekend
with all its reminders of how naive she'd been at
eighteen. More than naive: disposable, rejected,
mocked.

To stop her destructive train of thought, she
locked her attention back on Aaron, who was collecting the prescription from the printer. She'd
quizzed her parents last night when she'd arrived in Abbotsford, learning that he was still
decidedly single, despite an almost constant cam-

paign to lure him into a relationship by the village matchmakers and every hot-blooded single woman in the region. He also sent hearts and ovaries aflutter with his fanatical devotion to his little boy.

She observed him out of the corner of her eye and exhaled a discreet sigh; his magnetism, his maturity and dependability were exhausting. She was, after all, only human.

He signed the prescription and stood, passing it over to Gabby's mum. Stella perved another glimpse of his sexy backside, which looked as good in today's chinos as it had in Friday's jeans. She decided he was too perfect. There must be a catch, not that she was worried for herself. If he kept his word and applied for her transfer, she'd soon be away from his particular brand of temptation. But the local women deserved a fighting chance at resisting him, surely.

As Gabby and her mum stood to leave, there was a tap at the door.

Karen, the practice nurse, poked her head through the opening, her face serious. 'Aaron, we've just had a walk-in. It's urgent—can you come?'

Aaron excused himself to their last patient and nodded to Stella, indicating she should follow him. They hurried to the adjacent treatment room.

Stella's adrenaline spiked. She forgot all about fancying Aaron, about being back in Abbotsford, about everything except assisting the person in need of urgent care.

Inside the treatment room, a man in his early sixties sat perched on the examination couch, his fingers curled over the edge with a white-knuckled grip.

'Keep the oxygen mask on, Stan.' Karen replaced the mask over his nose and mouth. 'He's had chest pain since he woke this morning,' said Karen. 'Oxygen sats are ninety-two per cent.'

Aaron rushed to the man's side and took his pulse.

For a split second a flash of recognition gave Stella pause—the patient was Stan Mayfield, Harry's, uncle—but one look at his grey complexion, the sweat beading over his skin and his laboured breathing and she flew into action, wheeling the ECG machine she spied in the corner of the room over to the bedside.

'Call an ambulance, please, Karen,' Aaron requested calmly, encouraging Stan to lie back on the couch while he unbuttoned his shirt. That completed, he took the stethoscope from around his neck, placed the earpieces in his ears and moved the diaphragm over Stan's chest in order to listen to the heart and lungs.

'Does the pain radiate anywhere else?' asked Stella as she stuck electrodes to Stan's sternum, left chest, wrists and ankles in order to obtain an electrical trace of the heart.

Stan nodded, his eyes wide, terrified. He held up his arm, clearly too breathless to speak but indicating that the pain was spreading down his left arm.

Stella tried to comfort him with a hand on his shoulder, compassion nudging aside her adrenaline and automatic actions.

'I'm worried that you're having a heart attack, Stan,' said Aaron, his gaze flicking up to collide with Stella's. 'Dr Wright is going to take an ECG, and I'm going to give you some aspirin and something for the pain. Remind me, are you allergic to anything?' Aaron moved to the locked drugs cabinet and inserted the key from the set he kept clipped to the belt loop of his trousers.

Stan shook his head as Karen re-entered the room. 'Ambulance on its way.'

'And the only medication you're on is the anti-hypertensive I prescribed last month, Stan, right?' Aaron confirmed.

Another nod.

Stella pressed the button to take the ECG. Her respect for Aaron flew through the roof. Could he recall the medical and drug history of each of the two thousand patients registered to the practice? He'd grown up in this village. He lived here with his family. He likely knew everyone. Stella could understand how that could be an asset.

And sometimes, as in her case, a curse.

'Some aspirin, please, Karen, and morphine,' said Aaron, leaving the drugs to the nurse and joining Stella to look at the ECG tracing the machine produced. Stella pointed to the obvious ST elevation on the electrocardiogram, indicative of cardiac ischaemia. Aaron met her stare and nodded his agreement.

Stan was indeed having a heart attack.

Karen handed over the syringe and vial of morphine, which she and Aaron checked together, while Stella inserted an intravenous cannula into the vein on the back of Stan's hand. With the painkiller administered, Stan's pallor improved, his agitation lessened and his respiratory rate dropped closer to normal.

Stella stood back, feeling suddenly out of place, out of her depth, even though she knew she could have diagnosed and treated the medical emergency independently had Aaron not been here. Her bewilderment wasn't about the medical emergency. It was the wake-up call of treating someone she knew from her past life. Her pre-London, broken Stella life. A life she never wanted to revisit, but here she was anyway.

Stan had shown no sign that he recognised Stella, but seeing him again reminded her of that deceived, guileless girl she had been. She might have reinvented herself in London, taken her heartache and pretended it didn't matter, become a carefree party girl too happy-go-lucky for relationships. But the reality was that it had hurt too much to be eighteen-year-old Stella. And back here, her worst fears solidified.

She would always be that artless version of herself in Abbotsford.

The ambulance arrived, a flurry of activity as a brief history was shared and Aaron swiftly completed the paperwork and then called ahead to the accident and emergency team to let them know to expect an acute myocardial infarction.

The drama dealt with, a wave of shivers struck Stella as the adrenaline dissipated from her system.

As if he noticed her shaken composure, Aaron took her elbow and led her to the staff room.

'Time for tea,' he said in a no-nonsense tone, ushering her inside the deserted room, which was comfortably furnished with sofas, a flashy coffee machine and a reassuring array of healthy-looking potted plants.

Aaron wouldn't have missed her freak-out. He was a smart, perceptive, intuitive doctor.

He would ask questions. If he were any other man she might offer a full explanation.

Only, to him, there was none of her ugliness that she wanted to expose.

CHAPTER FOUR

'YOU DID VERY well this morning,' Aaron said, dropping her arm and flicking on the kettle. 'Tea or coffee?' He opened a large jar and placed an assortment of biscuits on a plate and then deposited them on the coffee table in front of Stella.

Stella craved the return of his touch, his warm, capable hand giving comfort she hadn't expected, even though it was probably just his doctor's compassion on display. But ever since that very first handshake back in London she'd battled this fierce attraction.

'Tea please.' Her voice sounded embarrassingly timid. She cleared her throat and reached for a chocolate digestive, needing the blood-sugar hit after the shock of seeing someone she knew, albeit from her past, in an acute medical emergency.

Poor Stan.

Perhaps it was the realisation that if Stan still lived locally, it was likely that Harry and Angus did too. Why was that only now occurring to her? She should have asked her parents if her ex was still living in the next village. What if they walked through the door one day? What if she bumped into them around about? She was over Harry, but that didn't mean that she wanted to relive his offhand dismissal, how easily he had cast her aside.

'Are you okay?' Aaron took a seat next to her so they both faced the stunning view of the rolling hills and a scattering of honey-coloured stone cottages for which the whole area was known and adored.

Stella nodded, taking a grateful sip of her scalding tea and reasoning that, after nine years, she might not even recognise eleven-year-old Angus.

'Yes. Sorry… I just…' She took a deep breath, sifting through her emotions in order to best explain herself without giving too much away to a man who unsettled her, made her crave his approval and his touch. A man she knew instinctively that she would struggle to keep at arm's length, as she normally could with men she found attractive and compelling. Not that she had ever found a member of the opposite sex this compelling.

She met his concerned stare, her mind trying and failing to come up with a good enough excuse for her behaviour. She didn't want Aaron to think she was…unhinged or unprofessional. But nor did she want to inform or remind him of her past errors of judgement, the consequences of which had played out publicly on the Abbotsford stage.

'I understand,' he said in his reassuring voice, his eyes searching and soft. 'Seeing acute medical emergencies in the community is nothing like dealing with them in hospital, where you are part of a team and have every imaginable drug and medical device to hand. You'll get used to it. And you were still part of *our* team.' His mouth stretched into a sympathetic smile that made her feel worse.

She wanted him to look at her the way he had in the pub on Friday. With heat and speculation and challenge and clear interest.

He took a biscuit, polishing it off in two bites. How could watching a man eat a biscuit be a turn-on? A bubble of light-heartedness filled Stella's chest, a miraculous feat considering the way her emotions had to-and-froed this morning.

She shook her head to both clear the erotic image of Aaron eating a chocolate digestive and to contradict his assumption. 'It's not that… I mean, you're right; it is different.' Just not in the way he meant.

She'd visited her parents here over the years, of

course, usually for just a few days, and each time she had feared the possibility of being recognised or seeing someone she knew who was linked to her ex. But this was different. Her placement with Aaron meant living here for an extended period. No matter how much she'd tried to prepare for her return to Abbotsford, she had been unexpectedly rattled by seeing Stan.

She looked up, met Aaron's quizzical stare, her stomach churning anew. 'It's just that I know him. Well, knew him. Stan. Mr Mayfield. It was a bit of a shock, that's all, although I don't think he remembers me.'

'Oh… Well, you're not really a local any more.' His teasing smile was designed to lighten the mood, she could tell. But, overcome by being back in a place associated with her most painful and humiliating memories, Stella swallowed down the absurd urge to cry all over him and his snuggly jumper.

He sensed her distraction, his expression becoming serious. 'You know, I'm a good listener, if you wanted to talk.'

She met his calm blue eyes, her pulse pounding at the realisation that despite their differences, despite how she felt about this traineeship and working with him, she respected him as a doctor. She even respected him as a man. Having been on the receiving end of it, she tried never to indulge in gossip, but you could hardly move in Abbotsford without hearing someone compliment Aaron Bennett, awesome single dad, brilliant GP and all-round nice guy. And now that she'd spent time with him, she understood the hype.

She didn't want to confide in him, except he had that bedside manner people warmed to, drawn into a confessional aura that made you believe that your secrets would be safe in his hands.

Would he understand how simply being back here reminded Stella of her worst pain and her biggest regrets? How, after Harry's betrayal, she'd vowed that she'd get smart, be done with relationships and never make herself that vulnerable to pain again?

If he hadn't touched her arm again, she likely would have kept the lid on the most shameful time in her life. But he did touch her, his fingers flexing on her forearm as if he couldn't help himself.

'It's okay,' he said in a low, soothing tone.

Stella's body shook from the collision of panic and desire. She sighed. She did owe him some sort of explanation after he had plied her with chocolate.

He probably knew the gossip version of the scandal that had driven her so far away from home, anyway. Better that he heard her side of events rather than that of the village grapevine. Better that she explained herself rather than give him the impression that she couldn't deal with her job.

Tired of tying herself up in knots, Stella took a deep breath. 'Before I moved away, I used to date Mr Mayfield's nephew.' She searched his blue eyes to ascertain if he already knew that information, seeing only mild surprise.

He nodded for her to continue, his hand slipping from her arm, his intent gaze clear of judgement or morbid curiosity. 'I don't think I know Stan's extended family. Most of them are registered at the practice in Cheltenham, I believe.'

Relief left Stella on a long exhale that Harry and Angus were unlikely to be patients of Aaron's. She wanted to say more, but for her sanity, for her pride, she needed to steer things back onto a professional footing.

'How do you deal with it?' Stella asked, feeling marginally better for the tea and biscuit. Only now that her adrenaline had waned, she became hyper-aware of Aaron once more, his warmth next to her, the solid physical size of him, his calm, unfazed disposition. Why did all of his attributes add to his charms?

'Deal with what?' His mug, which was emblazoned with the words *My Dad is a Superhero*, made her lips twitch with an indulgent smile that tugged at her heartstrings.

She tried to imagine him as a father. He still carried that air of confidence he'd had as a young man, gadding around the village in his vintage sports car, bringing home a bevy of besotted female nurses only too willing to be the woman of the moment and causing a few rolled eyes in the post office.

'Living in such a small community,' she clarified. 'You know everyone you treat and they know you. Your past. Your mistakes.'

Stella shivered as she recalled walking into the village shop soon after the rumours of her split from Harry had begun, hurtful, soul-crushing lies that had only added to her heartbreak. Unbidden, the worst of the tittle-tattle surfaced from her darkest memories.

Has she no shame, splitting up a young family?

She's very young, but then, she should have known it wouldn't last.

Of course he would go back to the mother of his child.

Stella hadn't been the other woman, she'd just been deceived and double heartbroken. If only she'd had two hearts to absorb the devastating impact.

How could people believe that she'd stolen her

ex from his baby mama when the reality was the opposite, that Harry had lied to Stella and strung along both of them? She had tried to ignore the stares, the loaded silences, to enjoy her last summer at home before leaving for uni. After all, she knew the truth. Her family knew the truth. Harry knew the truth.

And that had been the worst part. The piece of Stella still in love with him had hoped, dreamed, prayed that Harry would set the record straight in the community and come to her defence.

Only he hadn't. His disloyalty had amplified the pain of his rejection.

'That's true,' Aaron said, watchful. 'But everyone makes mistakes. We're all human.' His eyes clouded, perhaps with his own memories.

Stella's human fragility had certainly taken a battering nine years ago. Confused, raw and trying her best to put on a brave face for her parents, she had left for London, where, after crying every night of Fresher's Week, she realised that she could become someone new. A clean start where she called the shots.

She had left sad Stella behind and never looked back. Until now.

'So how do you distance yourself?' she asked, keeping things work-focused. 'How do you socialise with people that you know intimately? As a doctor, you sometimes see people at their worst. How do you then make conversation in the pub as if you're just another acquaintance?' Wherever she worked as a GP she would need to master this skill. She definitely needed it here.

Aaron brushed a biscuit crumb from the leg of his chinos. 'I have a young son, Charlie, so I'm not too much of a regular at the pub.' He quirked his eyebrows, his smile, the intensity of his stare reminiscent of his playfulness on Friday. 'As you already know, my nightclub days are over.'

Stella laughed at his attempt to lighten the atmosphere.

'But you're right.' He placed his mug on the table and leaned forward, resting his elbows on his knees in the way he did when he talked to the patients. 'Being a country GP has its challenges and limitations.' He spread his hands in a gesture of vulnerability. 'I only have a few close friends that I trust with my personal stuff, together with my family. Otherwise, I try to be a private guy. Most patients respect that, even here in a small community.'

'Don't you find it…lonely? Isolating? My experience of growing up here is that everyone knows your business. I found it claustrophobic.' She needed to shut up, but he was so easy to talk to.

Recalling his sad expression earlier, Stella wondered if he was lonely personally too? Five years was a long time to be alone. She shouldn't care about his solitude, about the fact that he was probably still in love with his wife. She had no desire to think of him in any way beyond strictly professional. Except her body hadn't read that small print. It lit up when he was close, craving those casual infrequent touches or the clash of his expressive eye contact.

Stupid Stella.

It was never going to happen. She worked for him and he would consider her too young. They couldn't be more different. He was the country mouse to her town mouse. He had a son and Stella wasn't sure that she even wanted children. She certainly wasn't on the lookout for a relationship, so his loneliness or lack thereof was completely irrelevant.

Only all weekend, while she'd spent time with her sister Darcy doing some of their favourite London things as a farewell—a spot of shopping on Carnaby Street, a trip to their favourite Knightsbridge tea shop and cocktails and dinner at a funky basement club in Mayfair—she hadn't been able to stop thinking about Aaron Bennett.

The real man twice as attractive as the fantasy.

Oh, no…this was bad. Her crush had no business reawakening, especially now when it came in adult form, complete with sexy daydreams and impossible cravings.

How dared he be so sexy? So distracting? So... Aaron?

'All GPs have to be good at compartmentalising,' he said, dragging her mind from the gutter. 'Once I leave the practice, I try to forget work and switch on the other parts of myself. Charlie helps me with that. Five-year-olds need lots of attention.' He grinned in that indulgent way that told Stella he loved being a dad.

Stella's rampant imagination saw Aaron the father: playful, nurturing, patient. Why was that so unfairly arousing? And how could she switch it off? He was a dad, like Harry. Another red flag she should heed. After failing to be enough for one man, despite her bond with his son, she had no desire to find herself unfavourably compared to Charlie's mother, Aaron's wife.

He stood, collecting the mugs and loading them into the dishwasher. Break time was over and Stella needed to pull herself together and stop lusting after a man she didn't want.

'At the end of the day,' he said, his eyes haunted and vulnerable as he returned to the conversation Stella had all but forgotten, 'we all have regrets and we're all entitled to privacy. Remember that.'

He left the room, leaving Stella more conflicted than ever. What regrets was Aaron harbouring and how could she hold herself distant, as he advised, until she could flee from both the way he made her feel reckless with need and the way he reminded her of her own bitter mistakes?

CHAPTER FIVE

AARON PULLED AWAY from the kerb, all too aware of how Stella's light floral scent filled his car and his growing obsession with the way she smiled, her happiness and how she made *him* feel: as if a part of him he hadn't even realised was missing had returned and wanted to steer the ship.

Well, there was no way he would allow his libido to take charge. She was fifteen years younger than him. His trainee.

But it was more than mere attraction, as rampant as that was. As much as he respected his GP partner, Toby, Stella seemed to bring a breath of fresh air and renewed energy to the surgery, as if she'd flung open the windows to invite in the cool, autumn-scented air.

On her second day Stella had again sat in on his morning surgery, impressing him with her astute diagnostic skills and the way she questioned everything, wanting to learn as much as she could from the experience, when he knew her heart wasn't in this particular placement.

She seemed to have recovered from her minor wobble after treating someone from her past. It was only when she'd questioned him about keeping a professional distance from the patients he lived alongside that Aaron realised how out of her comfort zone she was here in what he considered a little corner of paradise, a place he was privileged to live and work. That she had rocked up anyway and was giving the job her all showed her tenacity, determination, courage.

But what had made her feel claustrophobic all those years ago and was it anything to do with this ex she had mentioned? He wished she'd opened up to him more, confessed the deeper reason she was so spooked. Yesterday he hadn't wanted to push her too hard, to pry. He'd even resisted asking his parents if they remembered Stella from nine years ago. No one liked to be the subject of gossip—he understood that on a personal level.

After Molly died he had been the talk of the town for a while. Fortunately, he had been too consumed by grief and guilt to care. He'd had Charlie to focus on.

Aaron cast a side eye at Stella, who sat in the passenger seat, reconciled that she would tell him what she wanted him to know, if and when he earned her trust.

They'd just finished a house call and were now headed back to the practice for afternoon surgery.

'I remember Mrs Taylor,' she said, glancing at him with a relaxed smile. 'She used to be a music teacher at the school, didn't she?' Her voice carried a tinge of sadness, compassion for the retired woman, who was receiving chemotherapy for stage two ovarian cancer.

'Yes. She taught me piano for a while, actually.' He smiled in her direction, reluctantly returning his eyes to the road, because the green blouse she wore today brought out the sparkle in her eyes. He didn't want to crash because he couldn't stop staring at a woman he should not be thinking about that way.

'Do you still play?' The curiosity in her gaze heated the side of his face. To look at her would be to confirm what he'd see in her expressive eyes, what he felt growing stronger within him every moment they spent together and most of the moments they were apart: a constant, undeniable lure he was struggling to keep at bay.

But fight it he must until a new placement could be found and she moved back to London.

'A little—I'm trying to teach Charlie "Twinkle, Twinkle, Little Star".'

'That's adorable.' As he caught her lips curling into that wondrous smile of hers, he recalled what he'd come to think of as their *moments*, because this felt like another one.

What the hell? He should be convincing himself that he'd been mistaken, that a woman like Stella would have no use for a man like him. Except he couldn't forget their spark of chemistry on Friday night when she'd uttered a low challenge, for his ears only.

'See you Monday, boss.'

Her proximity when she'd leaned close to taunt him had set his body aflame for the first time in years. The shock that he had seriously considered kissing her was profound enough to render him on his best behaviour since.

But then they'd shared their second moment in the staff room yesterday when she'd haltingly confided in him about her reservations about returning to Abbotsford. Their differences, their working relationship...none of it had mattered in the face of her vulnerability. He had wanted to know exactly what made her tick, to understand her fears and dreams, to be alone with her. Not as her supervisor; not as Dr Bennett. Just Aaron, a man who'd, out of nowhere, reacted to this woman and needed to sort fantasy from reality in his mind so he could return to normal.

Well, his new normal anyway, the suspended

state he'd inhabited since Charlie was born: get through each day knowing that he'd done everything he could for his son. Mostly that meant putting his own needs second, but that was a small price to pay for the mistake of his past.

Dragging his gaze from Stella's profile and from all thoughts of shared moments, he returned his thoughts to his son.

'I just need to make a brief stop to pick Charlie up from school before we head back to the surgery.' His responsibilities grounded him once more. Fatherhood had become the best role in the world. That his libido felt nineteen again paled into insignificance, especially as it was directed at this particular woman. He wasn't a teenager, or in his twenties, or even in his thirties. Stella Wright needed to remain off limits, because not only had she reawoken his sexual urges, she had also reawakened his guilt.

Aaron didn't deserve such light-hearted and frivolous feelings as lust after letting down Molly and Charlie in such a devastating way. He'd had his shot at happiness. He'd had it all and his wife, his son's mother, had died because he had been careless.

'Of course. No problem.' she said.

Normally Aaron managed to drown out his self-recriminations. But today, perhaps due to

Stella's presence, memories gripped his throat in a choke hold.

Charlie's conception had been an unplanned slip-up. He and Molly had only been married a few months, and they had both wanted to wait a couple of years to start a family. She'd just opened her interior-design shop in Cheltenham and they were enjoying married life together, decorating the run-down old farmer's cottage they'd bought, establishing Aaron's growing practice, living the life of a couple before children.

Then one giggly, wine-fuelled night, a shortage of condoms and a miscalculation of Molly's likely ovulation date had changed everything. Nature had overtaken their careful planning.

Oh, they'd both been excited about the baby after the initial shock. They'd made new plans to share the parenting responsibilities so they could still both commit to their respective careers. But with Molly's death, his guilt and shame had roared to life. Aaron should have known better. He was a doctor, for goodness' sake. He should have been more responsible. Not only had he lost the woman he loved, but also his recklessness had condemned his son to life without his wonderful, kind and funny mother. Every child deserved to know both of their parents. If he'd been more careful, if Molly had become pregnant a few years later, as they'd planned, perhaps she'd still be alive.

Oh, he understood on an intellectual level that the rare postnatal complication she had suffered had nothing to do with timing. But his wisdom didn't help. His beautiful Charlie, with his mother's energy and sense of mischief, served as a constant reminder of Aaron's deepest regret.

'Does he enjoy school?' Stella asked.

He seized the lifeline, wondering how long he had been silent.

'He loves it.' Aaron forced himself to smile, to return to the present moment. To be what he needed to be: Charlie's dad. 'Walking home has become our routine, boys' time where we chat about our day before I have to head back to work for a few hours.'

'Perks of being the boss.' Stella smiled as if infected by the image of his rapscallion son, who was active and full of probing questions. Then she quickly looked away, out of the window, her expression falling contemplative as if she had suddenly remembered that she didn't actually like children. But that couldn't be true. He'd seen her interact with a few at the practice. She was a natural.

'Yes. I'm very lucky to have a job near home where I can walk him across the fields after school.' Rather than rebel against life in Abbotsford without Molly and resent being the much talked-about widower, Aaron was endlessly thankful for this close community. They had rallied around him and his newborn son when they'd come home from the nearby hospital. Baked goods and casseroles had arrived on the doorstep with reassuring regularity. Offers of babysitting had flooded in. As Charlie grew, people delighted in seeing him out and about, always cheerful and engaging.

To Aaron it was heartening and bittersweet, as if Molly's death had made Charlie different, special somehow, when Aaron wished he could turn back time so his son had two parents.

'We're also lucky to have such supportive families near by. I'm never short of a babysitter.' He tried to repay people for their kindness and consideration by being the best GP he could be.

'So who cares for him after school?' Stella asked, her gaze wary as if she was only making polite conversation.

'My parents or Charlie's other grandparents; sometimes his aunt, Molly's sister.' Aaron had never mentioned to Molly's family that the timing of Charlie's conception hadn't been exactly planned. He didn't know what Molly had told them about her pregnancy. He was just grateful that they'd never once openly blamed him for their daughter's death.

He blamed himself enough.

'I'm glad you have help,' said Stella. 'Raising children is the hardest job in the world.' She expelled a small sigh that he wondered if she was even aware of.

She had spoken generally rather than with first-hand knowledge. As far as Aaron knew, like Stella and Darcy, the middle Wright sister, Lily, had no children.

'You're welcome to join us on our walk, if you'd like. Charlie has been asking about my new work colleague.' At the slight stiffening of her body he added, 'Or you can head back to the surgery and familiarise yourself with the cases booked for this afternoon if you prefer.'

He didn't want to force his rambunctious five-year-old on her if she only tolerated children, but nor did he want to exclude her, especially when he enjoyed every second of her company more than he should.

Stella chewed her lip, clearly dithering.

'Not fond of small children, eh…?' His stomach sank, although how Stella felt about his son didn't matter. He had avoided relationships these past five years, focused on raising Charlie. They were a two-for-the-price-of-one combination that would put many women off.

He cleared his throat, irritated by his foolish disappointment. He wasn't looking for a relationship. He and Charlie had a good thing going, a routine, stability. He wouldn't jeopardise that.

'They can be a handful,' Aaron joked, trying to lighten the atmosphere and rectify the direction of his thoughts. 'Don't worry, Charlie doesn't bite, but it's no big deal. I want you to see what life as a rural GP, something I know you don't aspire to, is like, but there's certainly no obligation on you to participate in my extra-curricular activities.'

She shook her head as if clearing a silly thought. 'No, it's not that. I like kids as much as the next person. I'd love to join you actually. I'd like to see how the school has changed since I attended, and I could do with a breath of fresh air. Aside from my parents, obviously, stunning autumnal days like this one are what I miss most about Abbotsford.'

She stared out at the view—there was one around every corner—her small smile wistful.

'Oh?' he asked, intrigued anew by her complexity. One minute she acted bored by the pace of life here—bemoaning the lack of nightlife, feeling claustrophobic—the next she seemed fully at home in the village where she'd grown up. It was almost as if she was fighting her natural inclinations, acting as if she didn't belong for some reason.

But why would she do that? Perhaps it was linked to the ex she had mentioned. But that was a long time ago. Surely she'd fallen in and out of love a few times since then, in her search for Mr Right?

'I used to ride a lot as a kid and into my teens,' she elaborated. 'I spent hours riding Gertrude, my pony, out for a hack through these lanes and across the fields.'

'Now, there's something you can't do in London.' He could imagine Stella ruddy-cheeked and mud-splattered as easily as he could imagine her in skyscraper heels dancing with her arms over her head in some nightclub.

He swallowed at the memory of her long legs and shapely thighs, a tight black dress... He shouldn't be imagining her at all.

She shrugged, as if she'd merely swapped one rush for another.

Aaron understood. He'd once been desperate to move away from the predictability and expectations of home, to spread his wings and experience a different way of life. But unlike Stella, he'd always known that he would end up back here. He'd been raised to be heir to the Bennett estate his parents currently managed, which comprised the manor house, farmland and a handful of rented cottages.

'Do you ride?' Stella asked.

He shook his head. 'But Charlie is desperate for a pony, ever since he saw that animated movie with the talking horses.' So far Aaron had managed to dodge that particular demand. He shook his head. 'Never going to happen.'

'Are you overprotective, then?' she asked, looking at him with that hint of fascination that warmed his blood and had him craving their next *moment*.

'I prefer the term vigilant.' He frowned. 'It's something I never understood about parents until I had my own tiny human to love and nurture and keep alive. You never want anything to harm them, not a scraped knee or a broken heart.'

His insecurities tightened his chest, as if he'd run too far on a frosty morning. What if he made a complete hash of parenting? What if Charlie grew up hating him for the error of judgement that had led to Molly's death? What if he lost Charlie too as suddenly and pointlessly as he'd lost Molly?

'You're right. You want the best for them, all the time.' She nodded as if she knew exactly how he felt. Again he thought Stella must have some first-hand experience.

Then as if realising she'd said too much, she mumbled, 'It certainly must be a lot of responsibility.'

'And joy. Laughter. A steep learning curve.' He hesitated for a second but then ploughed on.

'You sound as if you have experience of children beyond professional exposure.'

He wanted to understand her reticence for being here, part of the Stella puzzle that clearly brought her some sadness, and he sensed it was connected. It wasn't his place to ask any more than it was his place to wonder at the softness of her lips or the intelligent depth of her hazel eyes, but there it was all the same, like an itch he couldn't scratch.

Outside the school, Aaron parked the car and turned off the engine, aware that his breath was trapped in his chest while he waited for a clue to the parts of herself she kept well hidden.

For a second, her stare moved from his eyes, to his mouth. His mind immediately returned to thoughts of kissing her. Did she fancy him in return? Had she, late at night when sleep evaded her, imagined his touch and if they would be good together, physically?

Need roared to life, waking every cell in his body. But it went beyond lust. He liked Stella. He wanted to know her. He wanted those moments.

She drew in a breath, as if preparing to share some intimate part of herself, but at the last second, she seemed to change her mind.

'Not really,' she said.

An answer that only left him with more and more questions.

CHAPTER SIX

AARON'S HANDSOME FACE lit up as the bell rang and older children began pouring into the school yard.

'Here they come.' He jumped out of the car and strode over to the school gate, where a cluster of parents and older siblings waited. Stella exited the car too but loitered near the back of the waiting crowd, feeling as if she needed a hat and some dark glasses to conceal her identity.

Did anyone here know her? Or were the prickles of apprehension dancing over her skin merely a reaction to the fact that every moment spent with Aaron seemed to bring them closer together? Make him more relatable, more complex and more human than her stamina could endure.

As he had talked about his son, his expression and the tone of his voice, even his body language shrouded in vulnerability, she'd struggled to tear away her gaze. Stella understood his sentiments and concerns with every beat of her heart. She too had loved a little boy with the ferocity of a parent, even though they hadn't been biologically related. Aaron's clear devotion to his son had brought the feelings rushing back until she could barely breathe.

For a few indulgent but foolhardy seconds Stella welcomed the memory of that other little boy, from another time: Angus. The soft, silky tickle of his fine hair against her face, the adorable toddler scent that she loved to inhale—a combination of baby shampoo, playdough and banana—the innocence of his trusting embrace, his small arms clinging to her neck as if she'd never let him fall, hurt or even cry.

She couldn't bear to think that the toddler she'd loved as fiercely as if he were her own had pined for her, even for one second.

When Harry had abruptly called things off via a cold, unapologetic text listing the reasons she knew were lies—that she was too young for him, that he needed to put his son first and try to make it work with Angus's mum—she hoped for the two-year-old's sake that Angus hadn't missed her one jot, certainly not with the soul-wrenching grief she'd experienced for him.

With the pain fresh under her ribs, Stella willed the bittersweet memories away, blinking at the sting of tears. Angus hadn't been *her* little boy, even if, for a while, she'd felt as close to him as she had to his father, Harry, the man she'd fallen head over heels in love with that final year she had lived in Abbotsford.

She cast a furtive glance around to see if any of the locals were looking her way, but all she saw were the large number of interested glances cast in Aaron's direction by the mums at the gate. One even hugged him and dragged him into her little huddle of chatting parents with an air of ownership that had others rolling their eyes.

Before Stella could examine the hot flush of jealousy, there was a bustle of small people, a cacophony of excited squeals and the collective triumphant waving of art in the air as the younger classes emerged.

Aaron crouched down to the eye level of a little boy with sandy blond hair the exact shade of his own, a golden field of corn or the very honey-toned stone that made this region famous.

Stella's stomach did flips at the vision. They were so alike. And she had been correct in her prediction that fatherhood would increase Aaron's sex appeal.

Warm currents shifted low in her belly. Aaron the man and doctor was hot enough. The addition of his fathering skills placed him beyond tempting, a combination potent enough to make any red-blooded woman get in line for a shot at bagging a hot daddy doc.

But not her. She had no intention of *bagging* anyone. If only her body understood that where Aaron was concerned.

She should have headed back to the practice. Not only would she have avoided the discomfort of wanting to tear at his clothes, but also sharing this seemingly innocent everyday moment with Aaron felt like an intrusion somehow, as if she was inappropriately elbowing her way into his life the way her accusers had claimed she'd done with Harry.

Aaron turned to seek her out, his face still wearing the indulgent smile for his son. He waved her over.

Stella tried to pull herself together as father and son spoke for a few minutes. The boy glanced in Stella's direction, thrust both his backpack and creative work at Aaron and ran off across the playground towards the rear gate of the school, which bordered rolling fields that lead to Bennett Manor.

Stella joined Aaron, her pulse tripping over itself despite her attempts to stay aloof and unaffected, to deny her attraction, which grew more and more rampant by the hour. Becoming emotionally embroiled was something she normally avoided by only casually dating. It kept her distant so that she didn't feel or grow attached. In Stella's experience, which was admittedly limited, feeling only led to pain, inexplicable rejection, isolation.

'He likes to exert his independence by racing ahead,' said Aaron in explanation as they fell into step, side by side, following behind a highly energetic Charlie.

Stella breathed a sigh of relief that Aaron hadn't made a big deal of her presence, and that Charlie hadn't peppered her with a hundred questions on who she was and why she was accompanying his father on today's walk home from school.

She certainly had no answers for the boy. This might be the stupidest thing she'd ever done. Hadn't she learned her lesson with Harry and Angus?

'He is full of beans.' She smiled despite herself. She didn't want to feel anything for Aaron or his no doubt adorable son.

Pride shone in Aaron's sexy grin. Of course, it only heightened the blue of his eyes and dimpled his cheeks. She needed a barrier to his potency, a distraction, and she needed it fast.

'Does he take after your wife?' she blurted, more as a reminder to herself that Aaron was likely still in love with Charlie's mum.

He shot her a side glance, his face falling but quickly recovering as if he was well versed in discussing his loss.

Stella winced, hating that she'd voiced the first thing that came to mind. 'I'm sorry—I heard about her death at the time, from my parents.'

A flare of shame heated her cheeks, because she knew all too well how it felt to be talked about. 'It's a small village. Like I said, everyone hears about your business, don't they?'

'I guess you're right about that,' he said. 'And thank you. Did you know Molly?'

Stella vaguely recalled a tall woman with amazing glossy brown hair and a wide, infectious smile. 'Not really. My mum liked her; said she had a great eye for interiors.'

Aaron's lips curved, a return to that smile that made him instantly approachable, engaging and oh, so kissable. So inappropriate, given he was talking about his wife, the mother of his child.

Aaron glanced at Charlie, who had his arms outstretched like an aeroplane and was swooping back and forth across the field. 'He has her zest for life and her sense of humour.'

Stella tugged her coat across her chest against the dampness of the impending dusk, which had seeped into her veins.

She had once imagined that she'd found that type of connection, lasting love with Harry. Yes, she had been young, just turned eighteen when they met. But she'd fallen hard and become starry-eyed for the slightly more mature twenty-three-year-old who had driven a battered old Land Rover and would stand in the rain waiting for her to finish stabling Gertrude just so he could give her a lift home.

He'd swept her off her daydreaming feet, and when he'd confessed that he'd had a two-year-old son she'd been excited to meet adorable Angus. They'd spent so much of Stella's after-school time together that Stella had fallen in love with both of them. Twice the risk equalled twice the pain when it had ended and she had found herself instantly excluded, alone and grieving.

Then the rumours had surfaced. The gossip. How young selfish Stella had tried to steal Harry and Angus away from his ex, a woman Stella had never met, never even thought about, because Harry had never mentioned her. When he had dumped Stella, the truth emerged, Harry cruelly confessing that he'd never stopped sleeping with Angus's mum all the time he and Stella were together, and that they wanted to give being a family another try.

Stella had felt used, stupid, immature, as if for Harry she had been nothing more than a distraction, a stopgap, a way to make Angus's mother jealous and want him back. The worst part had been that Harry had simply dropped his bombshell and moved on, reunited with his ex and picked up where they left off as if Stella had never existed. As if her deep feelings, her love, were irrelevant. As if she were a nobody.

Realising that she'd fallen silent and that Aaron was watching her, she picked up the conversation. 'It must still be hard for you at times. Does he ask about his mother?'

Aaron nodded, his eyes darkening with shadows. 'There have been one or two tricky moments. Mother's Day, birthdays, Christmas. Other children's simple curiosity, prompting Charlie to think that he's different. I struggle with that.'

Stella's sentimental soft heart clenched for Aaron and his son. Children were naturally inquisitive and quick to sense that they stood out in any way. No matter how blessed and privileged your life, human beings were designed to fear exclusion. Stella knew what it felt like to be a curiosity here. To be the recipient of pointed fingers and whispered unfair judgements.

'And of course, being a single parent, I'm paranoid that I'm doing it all wrong.' Aaron glanced her way. 'How is my dad-ranking on the village grapevine?' His mouth was tugged by that self-deprecating smile she'd come to expect as predictably as the sunrise.

She reluctantly looked away. 'I think you're doing all right. I've never heard a bad word spoken about you. And you seemed fairly popular with the village mums back there.'

He tossed his head back and laughed. 'You're not jealous, are you?'

Stella found herself grinning at the delicious sound of his glee. Then she rolled her eyes. 'As if.'

'You sound disappointed that I'm not some deplorable villain.' He waggled his eyebrows and Stella couldn't help but laugh, too. He was right. It would be easier for her wayward desire and her Aaron crush if he acted a little more despicably.

'Just because we're two very different people, who want different things, doesn't mean I don't respect you professionally,' she said.

'Well, that's a start, I guess.' His mouth twisted in a half-smile.

Stella's gaze latched on to his sensual lips, increasingly erotic images of them kissing sliding through her brain.

In lieu of an ice-cold shower, she needed an antidote to his magnetism.

'Do you mind me asking how Molly died?' She didn't want to cause him pain, but there was a professional curiosity that she knew he'd understand. And more importantly, the fact that he was likely still grieving, still in love with his wife, should help keep her rampant hormones in check.

'I don't mind,' he said, his lips pressing into a flat line. 'It was a long time ago. She went into cardiac arrest soon after delivering Charlie. She'd barely even held him.'

Shocked, Stella stopped walking.

He raised his chin as if girding himself to utter the words, his stare strained but unguarded. 'Amniotic fluid embolism.'

Stella reached for his arm the way he had comforted her yesterday, horrified for such a tragic and unfair loss. 'I'm so sorry. That's rare, isn't it?'

Aaron nodded. 'They managed to revive her, but she never regained consciousness after the arrest.' His gaze fell to her hand on his arm as if disturbed by her touch.

'That's awful. Tragic.' She dropped her grip and started walking again, putting a few feet of distance between them so that she could breathe, pull herself together and stop thinking of him in a sexual way.

Their steps synced once more. This time Stella made certain to keep her distance.

'She was transferred to ICU,' he continued as if forcing himself to continue the tale. 'She died two days later.'

Chills gripped Stella's frame, her empathy and compassion drawing her to him to a dangerous degree. She hugged her arms across her chest, floundering and, for the first time in years, fearful. For herself, for how easily she could become embroiled in her feelings where Aaron was concerned.

'I don't know what to say other than I'm sorry again.'

Aaron shrugged, but Stella saw his pain lurking behind his eyes, which seemed to display his every feeling. 'It was a horrible time, obviously, but I couldn't dwell on the tragedy, the bloody waste and unfairness of it all with Charlie to look after.'

Stella swallowed, gazed over at his profile. He glanced sideways and offered her a sad smile. 'Don't worry; we're okay. Charlie and I are a team. Boys Club.' He raised his fist and pumped the air.

She smiled, trying not to remember how she had once been a part of Harry and Angus's team. Until she hadn't. Because it had all been an illusion. A joke where only she was ignorant of the impending punchline.

'And we are lucky in so many ways,' Aaron continued. 'That's the message I try to instil in him. He has many people who love him, and he lives in a wonderful place to grow up.'

'It is that.' Stella's smile stretched, a flood of nostalgic childhood memories warming her through.

For the first time in ages Stella indulged her imagination of her own future and how it might look. She'd spent so long avoiding emotional entanglement in order to protect herself, she'd never given much thought to her desires for a family. Did she truly never want children of her own? Did her job, a job she loved, really provide enough to fulfil her? Would she always be content with big-city life, even when her friends started to settle down and perhaps move away to raise their own families?

She had once wanted all of those things until Harry had belittled and humiliated her, forcing her to change.

She became aware of Aaron's gaze.

'Earlier, you gave the impression that you might have experienced village gossip in a negative way,' he said with a compassionate smile that made her feel exposed.

'Mmm, just teenager stuff.' Stella reared back from sharing too much. She'd kind of assumed that everyone, including Aaron, knew her business. But even in the few days she'd known Aaron on a closer personal level, rather than from afar, she deduced that he wouldn't toy with her emotions. He was too kind, too upstanding, too honourable.

With a sigh she hadn't realised she'd held inside since she first drove past the *Welcome to Abbotsford* sign, she offered him half an explanation. 'I was young. Naive. The ex I told you about yesterday—stupidly I fell in love. Trusted the wrong person. Made a fool of myself.'

'None of which are crimes,' Aaron pointed out with a small frown.

'No. But sometimes guilt or innocence is irrelevant, especially when the tale is juicier when the facts are omitted. But that's ancient history.' She tried to change the subject away from her. 'I'm not a heartbroken eighteen-year-old any more.'

'So you left Abbotsford amid a cloud of rumours. I can understand how that hurt, but you should know that I've never heard any of this before. I hope that reassures you that maybe the past is where it belongs.'

Of course, respecting people's privacy was a vital part of his role as a GP, but she had come to understand that discretion and integrity were inherent facets of Aaron's personality.

'I'm sure you could ask around for all the details,' she said absent-mindedly. 'There are probably lots of people who recall the *scandal*.' She made air quotes around the last word, with bravado. The last thing she wanted was for him to see her in a negative light, not when she worked for him and when her feelings for him were so conflicted.

'If you want me to know you'll tell me.' He stepped closer so that their arms almost brushed.

Something intimate passed between them, as

if they were the only two people in the world, trading their deepest, darkest secrets. As if they could become friends.

Except friends didn't want to know how their chums looked naked.

Stella cleared her dry throat, kept her eyes front.

They approached the low stone wall that bounded the house where Aaron had grown up. Stella had only been inside once for a Christmas party where all the village children had been invited to meet Father Christmas underneath the biggest Christmas tree Stella had ever seen.

She paused at the gate, clinging to her self-imposed boundaries. 'I'll...um...wait here for you.'

Aaron turned to cast her a speculative gaze. 'Okay, although you are very welcome to meet my parents. They'll probably remember you.' He smiled so that she knew he meant because she had grown up here rather than because she was still an infamous homewrecker.

Before she could make an excuse, Charlie came running from the back of the house towards them.

'Daddy. Grandma made spaghetti for dinner, my favourite.'

As if he'd completely forgotten Stella's presence, Charlie peered up at Stella from behind his father's muscular legs.

'Who are you?' he asked in that direct way that only small children could pull off.

'My name is Stella. I work with your dad.'

I also fancy your dad something chronic.

Charlie's blue eyes widened and his chest puffed out. 'My daddy is a doctor.' He stepped from behind Aaron's legs and struck a series of martial-arts poses as if fighting an invisible villain.

Stella hid her delight behind pressed-together lips.

'Are you a doctor too?' he asked, as if remembering that she was still there, an unknown grown-up who warranted investigation.

'Yes, I am.' Stella nodded, trying to unsee the undeniable resemblance, including matching dimples when they smiled, between father and son. Despite Aaron's concerns, Charlie was clearly a confident, well-adjusted and imaginative little boy, and, as Stella had predicted, adorable.

Her heart gave an involuntary lurch that she wanted to run away from.

'Are you kissing my daddy?' Charlie asked out of nowhere, as if this was a perfectly reasonable question for a new acquaintance.

Stella flushed hot, no doubt displaying a fetching shade of beetroot red. Could they both see how much she *wanted* to kiss Aaron? How the thought endlessly occupied her fantasies?

The man in question merely emitted a low, indulgent chuckle at his son's question.

But then his eyes met hers and time seemed to stop.

He arched an eyebrow, his eyes full of challenge. This was probably the look that had once lured all those pretty nurses to succumb to his charms, leap into his sports car and attend his infamous house parties.

She looked away from Aaron's intense, very adult stare. 'Um…' *Awkward.*

'No, I'm not.' Her skin prickled, too hot, too aware, too close to the man who clearly still possessed all of the moves.

Oblivious to the stifling cloud of lust and panic engulfing Stella, Charlie continued his explanation as if for the dim-witted adults present. 'My friend Johnny said ladies and men kiss. That's how they get babies.'

Aaron's eyes once more locked with Stella's as she issued a nervous laugh. He obviously shared her mirth, his mouth twitching in that sexy way that felt like a secret, unspoken adult communication.

As if granted permission to think about exactly how adults made babies, Stella acknowledged in a rush that she absolutely wanted to have sex with him.

Oh, no, no, no.

Could Aaron tell the direction of her thoughts and how turned-on she felt?

'Johnny doesn't know everything, Champ,' said Aaron, his intense stare still holding her captive as he ruffled his son's hair. 'Why don't you say bye to Dr Stella, and you and I will talk about babies at bedtime, okay?'

'Bye, Dr Stella.' Charlie took off at the speed of light, leaving a fog of thick, cloying tension wrapped around her and Aaron. Wave after wave of exhilarating lust buffeted her poor, weak body in the silent moments that seemed to stretch for ever.

This was very bad indeed.

'Johnny knows *everything*.' Aaron raised his eyebrows. His smile was cool, relaxed, but the expression in his eyes was beyond suggestive. Carnal. Intent.

Then his gaze swept to her mouth.

Stella's pulse buzzed in her ears. Was he going to kiss her?

Did he want to have sex with her, too?

Her feet shuffled, her senses alive with anticipation that she tried to squash. What the hell was happening? She couldn't seriously be thinking about Aaron Bennett's soft-looking lips, wondering if he kissed with the same all-consuming confidence that he wore as well as the fine wool jumper moulded to his deliciously contoured chest.

Kissing Aaron was not allowed. Sex with Aaron was the worst idea she'd ever had. Even standing here in a puddle of loaded silence with him was highly reckless.

Stella laughed another nervous chuckle. 'I'll…um…wait here.' Her voice cracked.

Aaron hesitated, his body inching closer. Then he sighed. 'Give me a few minutes to get him settled.'

She nodded, resolved. 'Then we should…um…get back to work.'

Even if he didn't, she needed the reminder that they were working together, that no matter how tempted, she would never know if Aaron's kisses would be demanding and animalistic or slow and seductive.

And she was one hundred per cent okay with that.

Wasn't she…?

CHAPTER SEVEN

On Friday, Aaron arrived at the village pub, the Abbotsford Arms, for the school fund-raising quiz. The Parents' Association planned to update the school playground equipment and he wanted to support the event. It had nothing at all to do with the fact that he had mentioned it to Stella in the hope that she too might come along.

As the warmth of the pub interior defrosted his cold cheeks and fingers, his gaze swept the patrons for the woman he couldn't scrub from his mind, even for a second. Because that moment by the gate had been a game changer. He could no longer deny how much he wanted her or the way she looked at him in return. With hunger.

Stella stood at the bar talking to another woman around her age. She wore skinny jeans that showed off her great legs and a chunky-knit jumper that couldn't quite hide the curves of her gorgeous breasts.

A slug of heat detonated in his chest, spreading through him as if his blood was laced with narcotics.

He paused near the door, collecting his thoughts and examining his obvious excitement. Ever since Charlie brought up kissing that day, he hadn't been able to stop imagining her lips against his, her taste, if she would make sexy whimpers in her throat as their bodies met.

Was he totally insane, or just deluded?

He scrubbed hand through his hair and tugged his scarf from his neck. He'd been quite good at this dance back in the day. Flirting, seducing, fun and frivolous sex. But what the hell was he thinking now? Aside from a couple of tame dinners that had ended with polite goodbyes, he hadn't dated since Molly's death. It had been a long time since he'd shared a proper kiss, or any other intimacy, with another woman.

He knew his abstinence wasn't entirely healthy, but he'd been so focused on raising Charlie, compensating for being his son's sole parent, that his physical needs had been the least of his priorities.

But Stella and her throaty laugh and her figure-hugging jumpers seemed to have bumped the demands of his sex drive up to the top of the list.

'You decided to come?' he said to Stella as he arrived at her side and took in her warm, soft scent. He kept his arms glued to his sides to stop himself from touching her: her elbow, her hand, that small freckle on her cheek.

Those same cheeks pinkened as if he'd caught her out, exposed how she too felt about the whole kissing plan.

'Yes.' She smiled. 'Do you know Amy? She runs the riding school.'

Pretending that he hadn't noticed the breathless quality of Stella's voice, he greeted the other woman with a warm smile.

'Of course, I recognise you now.' He'd once talked to Amy about gently introducing Charlie to riding. The kid never stopped talking about ponies and practically galloped everywhere. Aaron just hadn't plucked up the courage to take him along yet. He could almost hear Molly's reservations.

Wait until he's older...

'Amy and I were at school together,' said Stella, her tongue unconsciously swiping her bottom lip as she looked up at him with that searching stare that seemed to ask a hundred questions whenever their eyes met.

She felt it too, this continual force drawing them towards a collision, like gravity. But what should they do about it, if anything? He wasn't getting any younger and he was essentially her boss.

'Well done on dragging her back to Abbotsford,' said Amy to Aaron. 'I've just this minute persuaded her to volunteer for Ability Riding while she's here. Get this city girl back into the saddle, literally.'

Amy grinned and Stella rolled her eyes. But the glow of enthusiasm around her told him she was as delighted as her friend to be associated with horses again.

The urge to touch her, kiss her, intensified. Aaron's body was also keen to get back in the saddle, but they worked together. Even a temporary fling without emotions could complicate things.

'I'm not planning on being here that long,' Stella said with a concerned frown in Amy's direction. 'So don't rely on me long-term.' At Amy's look of surprise, she added, 'Aaron has applied for a transfer back to London for me.'

Reminded of her plans to leave as soon as possible, Aaron tried to swallow down the violent rush of disappointment that he had no right to be feeling. But it was a perfectly timed reminder that no matter how many moments they shared, no matter that he couldn't stop thinking about her, that he wanted to kiss her, touch her, hear her moans of pleasure, she would soon be out of here.

She'd made it clear from the start that this wasn't the practice, or the place for her. Only he'd started to see glimpses of how being here brought out different aspects of her personality, flashes of fond nostalgia.

No matter how well her desire to return to London fitted with his aim to stay emotionally detached, Stella has settled in well at Abbotsford Health Centre. She had a warmth, a compassion that made her an excellent GP. She knew many of the local families that his practice served. Aaron knew that, despite her time away in London and her reservations about this ancient gossip, she'd be seen as one of them if she ever decided to come home and work in the village for good.

He met Amy's eye and offered a resigned smile.

Sensing both Amy's and Aaron's confusion, Stella blurted out more of an explanation. 'It's been great to be back, actually. It's just that I've lived there for nine years. I've grown up there in many ways, and that's where I always saw myself established.'

She flashed vulnerable eyes at Amy. They were clearly good friends. Amy likely knew all about this local guy, Stella's ex.

'That's funny,' Amy said, 'because until Harry broke your heart, you always dreamed about living in a country mansion like the one in Aaron's family. You planned to keep chickens and pigs and grow vegetables, while being a doctor on the side, of course.' Amy smiled fondly.

Stella laughed, nodded and avoided looking at Aaron.

Protective urges built inside him like steam. This Harry guy was the ex associated with the rumours. What had he done to her? Was Stella still in love with him, still running away from her feelings? That would surely explain what Aaron found utterly inexplicable: why she was still single.

A stubborn lump lodged in his chest; it tasted suspiciously like jealousy.

'Would you like to join our team?' Amy asked Aaron, changing the subject. She indicated a man who waved from across at the bar. 'That's my husband, Mike, and it looks like he's found us a table.'

Aaron cast Stella a surprised look. 'You're doing the pub quiz?' He hadn't planned his own team. He knew enough people in the village to just rock up and simply join an existing group.

'Of course. I'm great at general knowledge.' She narrowed her eyes in challenge. 'Why so surprised?'

He grinned, glad she was once more flirting, joking and looking at him with heated stares. 'I thought clubbing was more your style.'

She shrugged, feigning aloofness. 'I'm a woman of many talents.'

'We need a fourth, as my sister can't make it.'
Amy said, subtly edging away, drink in hand.

Aaron had all but forgotten that he and Stella
weren't alone. They'd worked together all week,
each day becoming more fraught with sexual
awareness. He felt her interest, too. It spurred
his own. But he had to be sure they were on the
same page.

'I'd love to join you, thanks. If it's okay with
you, Stella.' Aaron searched her eyes.

He found only mischief and sparks as she
looked him over as if examining prime horseflesh. 'Mmm…it depends. What are your
strengths? Because first prize includes a spa day
at Hawthorne Manor, and I'm very competitive.'

Amy chuckled and left to join her husband,
leaving him and Stella alone at last.

Deciding that his life could do with a few…
temporary complications, he flirted back. 'I
also like to win and I have many strengths.'
He stepped closer, dipped his head slightly so a
flush stained her neck. 'But for the purposes of
a quiz, I'm good at history, sport and medicine,
of course, not that you need me for that.'

Her breathing kicked up, fast and shallow as
she stared up at him. Then she recovered. 'I'm
not sure I need you full stop.' She flashed a playful grin, the pulse in her throat visibly hammer-
ing away.

'Maybe not, but with you being such a city lover and me being heir to the local manor, I'm also something of an expert on country pursuits.' He let his eyes linger on her lush lips for a second longer than was polite. Away from work and the perceptive eyes of his five-year-old, he felt free to flex the flirting muscles he'd kept in check all week. He was rusty, not dead.

She laughed. 'Is that so? Yes, I recall the weekend bashes at Bennett Manor, the fields littered with wine bottles and poor deceased clay pigeons.' She sipped her drink, her gaze on him over the rim of the glass.

Heat sizzled along his nerves. If she was intent on leaving soon, she would no longer be his trainee. Clearly their age difference didn't bother her, so he shouldn't let it bother him.

'Amy and Mike will cover farming and politics,' she said returning to the matter of the quiz he'd forgotten existed. 'If I take the music and popular culture questions, I suppose you might complement us nicely.'

He grinned at her mock reluctance. 'I'm glad I can be of service.'

Taking his drink from the bar staff member, he followed her to join the rest of their team, his eyes trained away from the sway of her hips.

Sitting close to her around the small table, Aaron struggled to recall any of his general knowledge. Their thighs kept bumping and every time that happened their eyes met, zaps of awareness and small smiles uniting them. She was right; their subjects of strength couldn't be more different, but laughing, competing to be the biggest know-it-all and cheering each other on, it didn't seem to matter in the slightest. Aaron couldn't remember the last time he'd enjoyed a night out as much, and it was Stella who made all the difference.

'Yes!' she cheered as the quiz master announced that their team had won the quiz.

She jumped to her feet with her arms held triumphantly aloft. The other three of them joined her. Stella hugged Amy and Mark in congratulation and then Aaron found himself the next recipient.

Chest to chest, her arms surrounding his shoulders, he could feel the fullness of her breasts, the warmth of her as he rested his hand in the centre of her back, the excited pounding of her heart.

His senses went into overdrive as her scent bathed him.

She pulled back abruptly, laughed nervously as if she hadn't meant to include him in the celebration, had gone too far. But it was too late. His body had reacted to hers, remembered the feel of her and wanted more than a chaste hug.

When she flashed him an embarrassed smile

as they retook their seats, he saw the evidence in her eyes; she wanted him too.

Recognition that hadn't been there before filled the slim space between her body and his. Stella pretended to be unaffected but she could no longer meet his eyes and her hands were tucked under her thighs as if she didn't trust herself not to reach out.

Aaron sighed under his breath, desperate to get her alone. Perhaps he would offer to walk her home later. They needed to acknowledge this rampant chemistry before it burned out of control, before he did something stupid, before she left and he missed his chance.

'Dr Bennett, sorry to disturb you.' Someone tapped Aaron's shoulder.

He turned to see one of the village youngsters, a farmer's son called Ben. 'Can you come and check out Sam? His blood-sugar alarm keeps going off, and he's acting a little bit aggressively.'

Aaron rose to his feet immediately, tilted his head indicating that Stella should follow and strode after Ben. When he reached Sam, an eighteen-year-old diabetic well known at the practice, the teen was pale, sweat beading on his brow.

'Hey, doc,' he said, his speech slurred. The way he slumped against the shoulder of the friend sitting next to him told Aaron he was probably feeling dizzy or confused.

'Sam, have you eaten?' asked Aaron, making a quick calculation of the number of empty shot glasses littering the table and dividing it by the number present in the group.

Sam didn't answer. Instead he rummaged under his shirt to silence the alarm on his blood-sugar monitor, which was alerting him to what Aaron already knew. He was hypoglycaemic, likely a side effect of drinking spirits on an empty stomach.

He heard Stella direct Ben, the kid who had called them over, to fetch a glass of orange juice from the bar.

A girl to Sam's right answered Aaron's question. 'He hasn't eaten. We were going to get some chips later.'

'How many of those has he had?' asked Stella, indicating the shot glasses.

The girl blushed and winced, no doubt feeling somehow responsible. 'About five. It's his eighteenth birthday today.'

'It's okay. It's no one's fault,' Stella said to the girl.

She accepted the glass of juice from Ben and indicated to the others in the group, who now wore matching concerned expressions, to vacate their seats and clear a path to Sam.

While Stella encouraged Sam to sip some juice, Aaron discreetly examined the boy's blood-sugar monitor, adjusting the rate of insulin infusion.

Sam's hand shook on the glass as he sipped, now a docile lamb under Stella's care.

'I don't think he needs to go to hospital,' said Stella. 'But we should take him home.'

Sam stared up at her with grateful eyes as round as saucers.

Aaron nodded, taking in the worried expressions on the faces of his friends. 'He'll be okay, guys. But I think he's had enough partying for the night. What do you say, Sam. Time to go home?'

Sam nodded slowly, rising to his feet and taking Stella's hand to steady his balance.

'I walked here,' said Stella to Aaron, her brow pinched with concern.

'So did I.' Aaron glanced around for a friendly face who could give them a lift. 'He doesn't live far, but I don't think he should walk.'

'I'll take him. I'm the sober driver tonight,' said the girl Aaron assumed was Sam's girlfriend.

'Thanks. We'll come too,' said Aaron, 'and I'll call ahead and warn his parents to expect us.'

The journey was brief and fortunately uneventful, the silence only punctuated by Sam's repeated mumbled apologies.

'Don't worry—we've all been there,' Aaron

said, recalling what it was like to be a teenager growing up in a small village; the urge to push boundaries, experiment, party hard—all under the watchful eyes of people who knew your parents and remembered you as a baby.

'Never drink on an empty stomach,' added Stella. 'Even the pub grub at the Abbotsford Arms is better than nothing.'

She and Aaron shared a secret smile, that of two people with plenty in common, most of all an attraction it was now impossible to deny.

At Sam's address, they escorted the young man inside and spoke briefly to his parents, who were well versed in managing their son's diabetes. Aaron was strangely grateful for Stella's presence. She was young, relatable, and non-judgemental. Was it because she too understood what it was like to grow up in a rural community, where entertainment was scarce and fun was often what you made it? Or was it simply a symptom of his need to know her better?

Back outside, the night had taken on a bitter chill. Aaron turned up the collar of his coat and glanced at Stella, relieved to see her tug a woolly hat from her pocket and pull it on.

'Would you like to go back to the pub?' he asked, too restless to return now that the medical emergency was resolved. 'I'll walk you if you like.'

She shook her head, once again avoiding his eyes. 'No. I think I'll head home. It's been quite a week.'

'Never a dull moment.' He grinned. 'And you thought you'd be coming to a sleepy practice which catered only for minor farming injuries and coughs and colds.'

She laughed, rolled her eyes and bumped her shoulder into his arm. 'Point taken.'

Her touch, deliberate and playful, set his pulse racing.

Then she seemed to sober. 'Abbotsford has changed, or perhaps I've changed.' She kicked at a stone with her toe.

'Maybe both,' he said, knowing no one remained the person they were at eighteen. 'Come on, I'll walk you home.'

He took off in the direction of Stella's parents' house, which was only a few streets away. He didn't want to say goodnight just yet and she'd fallen into a pensive mood he wished he could eliminate.

'It's okay,' she said, catching up in two hurried strides. 'I don't need you to walk me home. I know the way. This isn't some dodgy end of London.'

Aaron shrugged, unperturbed. 'I'll make sure you get home safe, all the same.'

'Very old-school. Thanks.' She acquiesced, falling into step at his side, her smile returned.

'Are you suggesting I'm old?' There were still a few streetlights in this part of Abbotsford, so he could see the way her rosy cheeks matched the shade of her very kissable lips.

'Distinguished and experienced perhaps.' She cast him a thoughtful glance. 'And definitely responsible. Who'd have thought...?'

He laughed, delight bubbling up in his chest. 'You had fun tonight, despite the lack of dancing. It was good to see you enjoying the quiz.'

'I did.' She grinned, her eyes bright.

He wanted to pull her close and kiss her cold-looking lips until they warmed up. 'So, you definitely still want that transfer, huh?'

Distraction was what he needed. A reminder that, irrespective of his out-of-control attraction, she'd be leaving for London as soon as she could. Only that served to make him want her more. He wasn't looking for a relationship. It could be brief but perfect.

She nodded, but unlike all the previous times, she didn't seem quite as adamant. 'You were right—your practice is busy and varied.'

She smiled up at him in that teasing way of hers. 'You even arranged an extracurricular medical event at the pub to keep me on my toes,' she said about Sam's unfortunate hypoglycae-mic attack.

'Well, I think you've settled in very well. You're certainly a hit with our female clients.' He and his partner had often discussed the need to advertise for a female GP to join them. Why could he see Stella fill that post so effortlessly?

A dangerous vision.

'Is there no part of you glad to be back?' he asked, as desperate for her confidences as he was for her kiss.

'There is.' She sighed. 'But I also feel like I've outgrown this place. Last time I lived here I was Sam's age, devastated by my first major break-up, desperate to leave and be in a place where no one knew me.'

'So staying away was easier?'

'I guess. Of course, the last thing I want is to run into an ex who broke my heart. But I got over him a long time ago.' She raised her chin.

Aaron wondered at that. It was certainly some-thing she told herself. But who was he to judge? He still carried his own regrets of the past, un-able to let go of the responsibility he felt about his part in Molly's unplanned pregnancy.

'It's just that I built a life for myself in Lon-don,' she said wistfully. 'I left here young, naive, someone who thought she knew what love was. Then I grew up.'

Closer to her street, the lights had disappeared, so he couldn't make out her usually expressive eyes, but her body language spoke volumes—hunched shoulders, hands shoved in pockets, head dipped.

'I changed,' she said, glancing in his direction. 'I realised who I wanted to be and what I wouldn't tolerate, and London helped me do that.'

It made sense. Except he had seen how naturally she fitted in here. Was running still working for her, or just holding her back?

'I don't think a city has magical powers.' Aaron stepped closer, lowered his voice. 'I think you would have done those things anyway. You can be who you are wherever you lay down your stethoscope, Stella.'

A small frown pinched her eyebrows together as if she hadn't expected that he saw her so clearly. But she too must feel their connection.

'So you don't believe in love?' he asked, needing to understand the root of Stella's fear. 'Is that why you're still single?'

He was pushing, probing, but what if she was standing in her own way? He saw it in the pub, the change, the lowering of her guard when she hadn't been able to hide her delight at their win, but then, when he'd challenged her view of Abbotsford, she'd withdrawn, as if holding herself remote once more.

Was it just from him and their chemistry, or from this place where she'd experienced the pain of a failed relationship?

'Wow—now I see where Charlie gets his propensity for asking direct questions.' She pretended to be mildly offended but he could see that she was toying with him.

'I'm serious. You're smart. You have a good job, and you're attractive. I would have thought you'd be living with someone by now or engaged, even married.'

She stopped, stared, her eyes alight as if he'd divulged an astonishing secret. 'Attractive? You think I'm attractive, huh?'

He nodded, his feet locked in place to stop himself stepping closer. Sexy, inspiring, funny. 'Beautiful is probably more accurate.' So beautiful his chest sometimes ached when he stared at her unobserved.

That tension he'd now come to expect when she was close wrapped its tentacles around them, the air seeming to pulsate. She swallowed. She must have felt it too. But then she set off walking again, dodging him and his questions.

'I've been career-focused.' She stared down at her boots. 'I don't have time for dating. And you're single too.' She shot him an accusatory look. 'It's not a crime.'

He wanted to laugh, change the subject, allow her to make light of this. But more than that, he wanted to know her, to understand what was in her way.

'No, it's not,' he said. 'But I found love. I've been married.' His reasons for avoiding dating since were complicated.

'But you haven't been in a relationship since Charlie was born?' She glanced at him, the look in those hazel eyes of hers intrigued.

Aaron shook his head. 'As you saw on Tuesday, Charlie's a full-time job, a job I love.' He smiled as an image of Charlie laughing popped into his head. 'He's had a tough enough start in life as it is. I want him to know that he might not have a mother, but he's loved and important, the most important thing in my life. Dating would… complicate that.'

'I understand.'

'Sometimes I imagine that Molly's complications could have happened during the labour, that I might have lost Charlie too.' Now, why had he told her that? It was something he only ever allowed himself to think in the dead of night.

'I'm glad that didn't happen,' she whispered, as if sensing his vulnerability. 'And it's understandable to worry about introducing him to new people. It can be confusing for children to meet a host of prospective partners, not really knowing if they will be around long-term and what importance they hold. He's a fortunate little boy that you put his needs first. Not everyone is so conscientious.' Her mouth turned down, a painful shadow crossing her expression.

Aaron assumed that she would clam up again, but she continued.

'My ex, the one I told you about…he had a son, Angus. He was two when we got together, turned three during our year-long relationship. I spent all of my free time with them. I became very close to Angus.'

'And then…?'Aaron held his breath, an ache forming under his ribs for Stella's pain, because this was the heart of her fear, and he wanted it to have never existed, for her sake.

'And then nothing.' She kept her eyes facing forward. 'The relationship ended abruptly. One day I was collecting Angus from pre-school after I'd finished school myself, playing with him until his father arrived home, the next day I was… discarded as if I had never mattered to either of them.'

Aaron's fingers balled into fists. 'I'm sorry that happened to you, Stella.' How could her ex have been so cruel as to use her like that, throw her away like rubbish after she had given so much of herself to the relationship?

She violently shook her head, as if rejecting his empathy or willing away tears. 'The worst part was that I wasn't even given a chance to say goodbye to Angus, to explain my absence. I just hope that he forgot all about me quickly, that he didn't...pine.'

Because he couldn't stand not touching her any longer, Aaron scooped up her cold hand, tugged it, warmed her frigid fingers with his own body heat. 'You loved this little boy.'

She looked up from their clasped hands. He saw it written all over her face. This was the missing link, the child she had experienced, the reason that failed love affair had cut so deep. She had been doubly invested.

She nodded, her eyes glistening. 'I did. More than I loved his father, as it turned out.' She gave a humourless laugh. 'I worried for a long time after that Angus might have grieved for me the way I grieved for him, that he wouldn't have understood where I had gone and that it had nothing to do with my feelings for him.'

'I'm sorry that you had that experience.' No wonder she had run away emotionally when she left for university. She would have been grieving for the loss of two relationships, confused and rejected and wanting the pain to stop. It wasn't

Abbotsford that she feared. It was the pain she'd experienced here.

This Harry guy had clearly used her. Smart, emotionally astute Stella would have realised that, felt the sting of humiliation on top of her heartache.

As if collecting herself from a momentary lapse of weakness, she pulled her hand from his and shoved it inside her coat pocket. 'Well, this is me. Sorry for offloading my sob story onto you. Thanks for walking me home.'

Aaron's heart sank. Of course she would shield herself from this thing brewing between them. She'd been badly hurt. Rejected by a man like him. A man with a young son.

There was a light on in the porch of her parents' cottage, casting an orange glow that illuminated the cobblestone path and reached the small wooden gate, where they paused.

'No problem.' His voice felt thick with emotion. 'Thanks for your help with Sam. We've all been there. Hopefully his hangover tomorrow will give him plenty of time to reflect on his decision to drink on an empty stomach.'

Aaron hated the polite distance in his tone. A part of him wished he'd never discovered the depths of Stella's past heartache, wished for a return of the flirtation, the careless touches, the possibility.

But a bigger part of him wanted to hunt down this Harry fellow who had made a young, heart-broken Stella leave Abbotsford feeling as if she no longer belonged and...

No—Aaron wasn't a man of violence.

'You're welcome.' She placed one hand on the gate and looked up at him, her rapid breaths misting in the damp air as she loitered, saying goodbye but not moving inside. 'I'll...um...see you Monday morning, then.'

Still she hesitated.

Even though he told himself to proceed with caution because he didn't want to hurt her, some invisible force gripped him. Her display of vulnerability, the trust she showed him, the need to comfort her... He just couldn't stop himself.

Without questioning the danger of his action, he swooped in and pressed a chaste peck to her freezing cheek, telling her that he cared, that she hadn't deserved to be treated that way, that he valued the time she had committed to Abbotsford.

It was friendly at best. Only they weren't friends.

Although his lips had left her skin, he lingered in her personal space for a split second longer than was wise, hypnotised by the scent of her perfume. A lock of her hair tickled his cheek.

He was about to stand tall, move away—

his apology for crossing a line forming on his tongue—when she turned her face to his and their lips grazed.

It could only have been described as a kiss, no mistake. And she'd instigated it.

Fire consumed his nervous system, his body so rigid he thought he might snap and shatter like an icicle. But he wasn't letting this chance slip by without taking full advantage.

He pressed his lips back to hers, applied some pressure. His stare latched to hers, silently communicating that he'd heard her tiny gasp, that he'd take her mouth graze and raise the stakes, unleashing the desire that had been brewing inside him since he'd called her name in City Hospital's lecture theatre.

Instead of moving away or shoving him aside, Stella stepped closer, fitting into the curve of his body, which was bent over hers, a big spoon to her little spoon.

At the glow of arousal in her eyes, Aaron moved his lips against hers, parting, pursing, pressing home as if their rhythm was the most natural thing in the world.

But this was his first proper passionate kiss in five years. He was kissing Stella.

She whimpered, gripped the lapels of his coat, held him firm. He forgot about the fact that she was his trainee, that he was so much older than her, that he'd just learned what she had been through in the past, forgot everything but the sensation of kissing her and the way his body flared to life, his blood pounding, his hormones raging.

Drunk, high, dazed with desire, he wrapped one arm around her waist and cupped her cold cheek with his other hand, touching his tongue to hers, licking, tasting, deepening the kiss as if life itself depended on their connection.

Stella's fingers dug into his shoulders. Then she moved her hands to his hair, her fingers spearing through the strands and dragging him impossibly closer. Their bodies meshed together, from lips to thighs. He felt every inch of her curves, her breasts, her hips, the heat between her legs. A grunt of satisfaction ripped from his throat. He pressed her up against the gate, the barrier allowing him to grind their bodies closer. His erection surged against her hip. She bucked and writhed, massaging his length between her stomach and his, torturing him to the point of combustion.

His fingers slid under her jumper, finding the soft, warm skin of her lower back. He swallowed her moan. He worried that his hands were cold, but she gripped him tighter, urged her body closer, begging with her body language for more.

And insanely Aaron wanted to give her exactly what she craved, right here on her parents' doorstep.

With a shove and a strangled moan from Stella it was over as quickly as it had begun. Cool air bathed his lips, which were parted to drag in brain-fuelling oxygen. He looked down, confusion dousing his euphoria as if he'd fallen into a waist-high snowdrift.

Stella's eyes were huge in the dark and glazed with passion, but she slipped from his arms and fumbled with the latch of the gate at her back.

'Goodnight, Aaron.' Her eyes spoke a million words—excitement, regret, maybe even a trace of that fear she must have developed after her last run-in with a single dad from Abbotsford.

Similar emotions recoiled inside him, a rush of shocking lust he'd thought he'd never feel again predominant. He should apologise for kissing her, only he wasn't sorry. He was glad that she'd taken the kiss from a friendly goodnight peck, one they could return from, to one that would likely keep him awake all night. His only regret was that he might have misled her with his passionate response, the last thing he wanted to do.

'Goodnight, Stella,' he said, rueful that Monday morning might bring recrimination and awkwardness at work.

He should be grateful that she had withdrawn from their kiss. Aaron had Charlie to prioritise and he didn't want to hurt Stella when they had no future. He'd had his chance at happiness. Five years ago, as he'd held his days-old son in his arms, he'd made peace with the fact that he didn't deserve another shot.

Except his lips buzzed in remembrance of her kiss, already craving a replay. He waited until she was safely inside before he began the pensive walk home, the conclusion dragging at his heels: that he should keep away from Stella. For her sake.

CHAPTER EIGHT

STELLA HADN'T DREADED a Monday morning as much since she attended Abbotsford Secondary School and all she had wanted was for the weekend to last for ever so she could ride Gertrude. Oh, she was keen to get stuck into a new week at the practice, but a big part of her, the part scared of how shocking and out of control her physical reaction to Aaron had been, wanted to scuttle back to London and hide just to distance herself from the memory of that kiss at her parents' gate. Except denial wouldn't work. The details of every touch, every gasp, every sensation were seared into her brain like a mnemonic she'd had to memorise at med school in order to learn the order of the cranial nerves.

Aaron kissed with the same efficient, unflinching confidence he displayed at work and out of work. She had never wanted it to stop. Only confiding in him about Angus and then kissing him…it had been too much. Too intimate. Too dangerous.

She'd sensed that Aaron too had reservations that went deeper than having to return home for the babysitter, as if they were both wary of crossing that line that would take them from colleagues to lovers. She'd watched him walk away, peeped through her parents' porch window, still haunted and turned on by his expression of both loss and desire, which had been etched into his face as he'd said goodbye.

Stupid Stella. She'd acted on her attraction and now she had to face the consequences.

Sucking in a deep breath, she tentatively tapped on his consulting-room door. There was no avoiding him today or avoiding what she'd done, because she had spent the weekend berating herself for starting that kiss and listing the repercussions for their working relationship. If only he weren't such a good listener, so perceptive and impartial. If only she could stop wanting him with a need that bordered on obsessive.

'Come in,' he called, his voice sounding way too normal for Stella's liking.

Feeling as if her legs were boneless, she entered.

Aaron was alone.

Bad, bad news—she needed as many barriers to temptation as possible.

He looked up, removed his glasses, his smile hesitant but his eyes lighting up.

Stella swallowed past her dry throat. *Act natural.*

'Do you have a minute?' Her voice broke as she tried and failed to stave off the flush of heat that crept up her neck.

Say no. Send me away. Tell me that we made a mistake that can never happen again.

'Of course.' His open, honest smile kicked up at the corners. It had the same effect as the intense, carnal expression he'd worn on Friday night when he'd rocked the ground under her feet and kissed her as if he'd been dreaming of doing so since the first time they spoke.

'As it happens, my ten o'clock cancelled last-minute. Come in.' He stood and Stella closed the door.

With her back to him she could block out the delicious sight he made. Dressed in another fine wool jumper, this one the shade of Scottish heather on a windswept moor, he looked edible. Definitely kissable. Other things too. Tempting, sexy, but ridiculously unwise things.

She turned, cemented her feet to the floor to avoid burying her face in that jumper, inhaling his scent from the soft wool and losing herself in his proximity, masculinity and mastery as she'd done at her parents' gate.

The warm room became vacuum-like and hormone-charged. Stella struggled for breath but tried to focus on the query she had in relation to her patient rather than on the man who had the ability to make her forget all of the reasons that she didn't date. Aaron wasn't the usual type she went for: guys out for a good time without strings. He was still grieving the loss of his wife. He had Charlie to consider. He was her boss.

'I need your advice,' she said. Yes, this was better. Keep things professional, pretend that the kiss to end all kisses hadn't happened and hope that he didn't want to discuss it/fire her/prohibit a rerun.

'I've…um…seen Mrs Cavanagh this morning.' She stared at her phone, the notes she'd made blurring.

'Ah, yes, chronic pain,' said Aaron. 'Tricky case—it was a bit mean of me to give you that on your first day of working independently.' He offered her a seat and then took his own, scooting it forward until their knees almost touched as he gave her his undivided attention. He'd done the same thing many times as they discussed patients or shared the same computer, only now it felt too close. An invasion of her personal space that shredded her peace of mind.

'Not at all.' Stella's stomach turned to jelly. She'd have been happy with only a fraction of his attention; perhaps then she would have been able to think.

So why didn't she scoot her chair back?

'Her history is complex but interesting,' she said, aware of the way her lips formed words and how he watched her talk, his gaze pinging between her eyes and her mouth, as if listening but also distracted by what they'd done on Friday night.

'I saw a similar case as an in-patient at City, actually.' Slightly breathless, she wet her lips, remembering those few soul-searing moments at her parents' gate and how he had made her feel eighteen again. Only it had been better than any kiss she'd experienced back then. Now she was a woman who knew exactly what she wanted.

'Three months ago you changed her medication,' she said, forcing her thoughts away from kissing and back to Mrs Cavanagh. 'She's been in tears this morning because she feels that nothing has helped so far.'

Aaron leaned back slightly and rubbed his chin while he pondered this newest development. Stella had to blink to break the memory of his stubble-rough chin scraping her face in the cold, dark night. Of the way he had groaned with pleasure, such a sexy sound. Of the way his manly body had completely engulfed her until she had wanted to melt into him.

'Do you feel she's becoming clinically depressed?' he asked, clearly faring better than her at keeping his mind on track.

Did that mean he was done with her, with whatever this was? Maybe he'd spent the weekend reconsidering his response to her rash kiss. Maybe it was just she who craved more.

Deflated by that conclusion, Stella nodded. 'I think so. She scores highly on the depression scale and she said that she hasn't been sleeping.'

'Okay, well, she recently lost her sister, so I'm not surprised that her pain has become harder to manage.' He looked at Stella with his Dr Bennett eyes, as if he hadn't kissed her until she'd almost orgasmed on Friday. 'So, what's your management plan?'

Stella hesitated. The kiss had changed their working dynamic. Where last week she'd have been confident to express her opinions, now she felt uncertain, as if she was pushing an agenda, being somehow manipulative.

No. The patient's best interests were all she cared about. Aaron would hear out her suggestions and be objective. He, after all, had been nothing but professional since she entered his room.

Stella pushed her hair from her flushed face. 'There's a newly appointed pain specialist at City Hospital who is having some success with a combination of traditional therapies and alternative approaches, like meditation. I think a referral may be warranted, but I wanted to check what you would do in this situation.'

'I agree—a referral is appropriate.' He quirked an impressed brow that made her feel ten feet tall. 'I didn't know about the new pain clinic, so thanks for the insider knowledge. And how will you manage the depression?'

'I offered her a first-line antidepressant, but she refused. She said she'd like to get the pain under control before she considers taking *any more tablets*. I gave her some information sheets on non-pharmacological remedies, exercise, sleep hygiene, et cetera, but I think she needs more than that. I also suggested that she talk to the practice counsellor, and there are some excellent guided meditations for chronic-pain management online.'

Aaron's smile widened. 'You've done everything I would have suggested. Well done. Make the referral to the pain clinic and mention the mood disturbance in your referral letter. They will re-discuss it with her, I'm sure, as the two so often go hand in hand.'

'Thanks.' Stella stood and made for the door, elated at her clinical management plan but also strangely disappointed that Aaron hadn't ravaged her on his desk.

She needed to get a grip. He wouldn't be unprofessional with a waiting room full of patients beyond the door.

She didn't get very far.

Aaron's deep voice brought her escape to a premature halt. 'I think we should talk about what happened on Friday night.'

Stella froze, turned, cast him a glance full of bravado. 'About Sam?'

Being deliberately obtuse seemed petty, but resisting him was hard enough when they discussed patients. Actually talking about that mind-blowing kiss might trigger another lapse of her judgement. Things were awkward enough. She was in enough trouble, wanted him too much to trust a single idea her weak brain formulated.

Aaron stood and her belly fluttered. 'No, about us.' His voice dropped an octave, his tone husky and intimate. Stella was reminded of the way he'd uttered the word *goodnight*—full of reluctance. Need. Regret.

'About the kissing.' He stepped closer, his eyes moving over her face slowly, thoughtfully, patiently.

Why couldn't she be as cool and collected? As mature and unaffected?

She shrugged, while her heart raced with excitement. 'Do we need to talk about it?'

Did she have the strength to talk about it?

She'd prefer to simply launch herself across the room at him and repeat the mistake that had ruined her for all future kisses.

He tilted his head, as if he saw straight through her protective disguise, his stare intent, ducking between her eyes and her mouth as if he remembered her taste and wanted more.

'You're right. We probably should just pretend it didn't happen.' He drew in a controlled breath that Stella wanted to disrupt. She wanted to turn him on, remind him how well they had fitted together on Friday, until he too felt conflicted and needy.

His suggestion was the sensible thing to do. The best way to resume what was left of their working relationship.

Except...

His eyes became so intense, she had to blink and break the connection. 'I don't want to hurt you, Stella.'

His honesty and integrity fanned the flames of her obsession. He was making it so hard to stay rational and detached.

'I wouldn't allow you to hurt me,' she whispered, entranced by the look in his eyes.

He raised a hand and cupped her cheek. The contact made her knees almost buckle, her body sway closer.

'I have a big problem,' he said, his voice full of gravel. 'I'm not looking for a relationship—'

'Neither am I,' she interrupted then gripped his wrist, keeping his warm palm pressed to her face. She knew what she wanted and what she didn't want. She didn't want a relationship, or to be hurt. But she sure as hell didn't want to lose his touch.

His pupils flared, the black swallowing the blue of his irises. 'But I can't help wanting you. Wanting to kiss you again. Wanting more.' His thumb swiped her bottom lip in provocation.

Oh, her too.

She sighed, closed her eyes, enjoyed the moment that felt like that weightless feeling at the top of a swing.

She opened her eyes. 'I want you too, but I'm not sure that it's wise.' The last few words came out as a whisper, totally lacking conviction. How could she be so weak? So led by her hormones? She dropped her hand from his as if to bolster her resolve.

But seriously, who cared about wisdom with chemistry this good? She'd be leaving as soon as her transfer came through. Surely she could indulge in her ultimate fantasy: one night with Aaron Bennett?

Question was: would she survive it?

His hand slid from her face and hung at his

side. 'No, it's most definitely unwise.' His lips flattened, and she wanted to snatch back her words. She wanted his touch back, his skin on hers, closeness. Combustion.

'Unless...' he said, one eyebrow quirked in suggestion.

She latched onto that portentous word. 'Unless?' The pleading sound of her voice caused a flush to her skin.

He watched her parted lips in silence for a beat or two, his features shifting through a gamut of emotions as if he too waged an internal battle of sense versus need.

'Unless we both want the same thing.'

She nodded, euphoric that they might be on the same page. 'Just sex.'

Simply saying the word clenched her stomach in anticipation, the memory of his mouth on hers, his thigh between her legs, his hardness pressing into her stomach reawakening her body's aroused reaction.

He conceded with a tilt of his head. 'No emotions. Nothing serious.'

The confirmation was all Stella required for her arguments to crumble. 'After all, I'll soon be leaving.'

'And I only have room in my life for Charlie.'

She wanted to sleep with him. Why not? Neither of them had any interest in a relationship, so they could keep feelings off the table. Her move back to London would physically distance her from any stupid ideas her body might have in craving more than one night in his bed. What was the harm? Their chemistry only grew, day by day. Soon there'd be no containing it. The sexual tension drawing them closer was almost inevitable.

They were going to happen, heaven help her.

He dipped his head, brought his mouth closer as if he could no longer hold back from kissing her, but he kept her waiting, giving her time and options she didn't want.

'Still think it's a bad idea?' His breath feathered her lips, his stare dark and seductive. That look would surely have lured many women under his spell and into his bed.

Stella's heart leapt against her ribs as she tilted her chin up, looked at him from under her lashes, her lips only inches from his. 'Probably,' she shrugged, 'and I'm done with things that are bad for me.'

Despite evidence that he still had the moves that had given him a heartthrob reputation, she could no longer fit him into the same category as her bad-boy ex just to deny how much she wanted him. Younger Aaron might have been a bit of a playboy, but mature Aaron was a community stalwart, a doting father, a diligent and compassionate GP. He was nothing like Harry, who, in starting a relationship with Stella, lying about the fact that things between him and his ex were irretrievably over, had put himself, his feelings and wants above those of both Stella and his own son.

Aaron put Charlie first.

Unable to stop herself, Stella leaned closer as if pulled by gravity, placed her palm in the centre of his chest, her fingertips flexing into his soft jumper registering the pounding of his heart.

A soft groan left him. His gaze slowly traced her features. 'The fact that you're looking at me with glazed eyes, dilated pupils and parted lips tells me that you know we will be so good together.'

The vulnerability haunting his eyes shattered the last of her crumbling resolve. She wanted him and she'd exhausted all of the excuses she used to resist.

She nodded. 'Just one night.'

He reached for her free hand, tugged it and wrapped his arm around her waist, shocking a gasp past her lips. Her breasts grazed his chest, darts of pleasure shooting along her nerves. Their eyes locked.

He dipped his head.

Her chin tilted, mouth raised, ready to surrender to his delirious kiss once more.

A shrill ring tone rent the air.

With a sigh Stella felt against her lips, Aaron dropped his forehead to hers, closed his eyes and growled in frustration.

Stella's breathing came hard. Arousal spiked her blood, its potency draining away as Aaron took the phone from his pocket. He straightened, keeping one hand on her waist, stared deep into her eyes as he answered.

'Yes, Penny,' he said to the receptionist on duty today.

Stella stood transfixed by the heat and desire and promise glimmering in his eyes. They spoke of a similar need ransacking her body, making her weak, needy, heedless of the consequences of wanting this particular man and ready to throw all caution to the wind to be with him one time.

'Your ten-fifteen is here.' Stella heard Penny's side of the conversation and took a step back. The loss of his warmth and the hard comfort of his body physically hurt. Disappointment drained her limbs of energy. She sagged, looked down at her feet and then held up her hands, palms out as she backed towards the door.

What had she been thinking? They were at work. It was mid-morning. There was a waiting room full of patients out there. She'd become almost completely carried away. Without interruption, she'd have kissed him and done who knew what else right here in his room.

As she instructed her desperate, weak libido to get a grip, Aaron ended the call, his eyes still laser-focused on her. That look was trouble, determination and resolve clear in the jut of his jaw.

'To be continued, Stella.'

Without comment, she scarpered, too turned-on and terrified to do more than nod.

By the end of her second week, Aaron was climbing the walls with exasperation to be alone with Stella. It seemed that every member of the local community had gone down with the 'flu, the seasonal spike earlier than expected that year. They had been swamped at the surgery, working late most evenings in order to meet the increased demand for appointments.

Outside of work he'd been busy too. Charlie had extra lessons for a swimming tournament and a mid-week after-school birthday party to attend. When Molly's parents asked if they could have Charlie over to stay on Friday night so they could take him to the car-boot sale two villages over on Saturday, he'd almost wept with relief and gratitude.

His first thought: to invite Stella on a date. A casual, nothing serious date. A drink in a quiet pub out of Abbotsford where they could talk, be alone, explore each other.

He missed her open smile and her playful sense of humour. Not to mention the hot promises they had made with their eyes at the start of the week when, to his utter relief, they had laid down the ground rules for managing their chemistry. And the torture had continued. Just because they skirted big circles around each other at work, succeeded in keeping their hands off each other, it hadn't stopped them practically torching the entire practice with longing stares and knowing looks.

Aaron pulled into the stable yard of Amy's riding school and parked his car. Stella had left work earlier, saying that she was going for a ride. Some of the regular Ability Riding children had missed their class due to the 'flu also ripping through the primary school, but the horses still needed to be exercised.

Instead of bounding from the car in search of Stella, his natural inclination, he paused, gripping the steering wheel as his doubts resurfaced.

As much as he didn't want to hurt Stella, neither did he want to disrupt the sense of contentment he'd finally found for himself and Charlie. He'd been as clear as he could, and she understood that his son came first. If they kept it about sex, as Stella suggested, there could be no misguided expectations.

He snorted, shook his head. He was overthinking.

This thing with Stella had an expiry date; she would soon return to London.

Tired of tying himself up in knots, Aaron headed to the stables and called out a hello. Despite the floodlit gravel car park, the buildings seemed deserted but for the horses quietly chomping hay. Perhaps he'd missed her. She hadn't answered his earlier text, which invited her out this evening, so he'd called in at the stables on the off-chance that she hadn't yet left.

His gut tight with disappointment, Aaron headed to the staff room he knew was at the back of the property. He'd once made a call here to examine an experienced rider who'd taken a fall and had a moderate concussion.

In his haste to see Stella he rounded the corner of the building and smacked right into her. His hands gripped her shoulders, to steady both her and himself as his heart thundered in relief and excitement.

'Hi,' she said, gripping his forearms, looking up at him with that secret smile she'd worn all week. A smile for him, for them.

'Sorry about that.' He smiled, pretended to be unaware of her shudder under his touch. Otherwise he'd want to pick up where they had left off on Monday in his office and kiss her until she was breathless and clinging to him and the restless energy twisting his insides vanished.

Her hair was damp at the ends as if she'd taken a shower. She smelled like a fresh meadow. He wanted to haul her close, kiss her as if the world was ending, put that glazed look of passion on her face and give her a new association with Abbotsford, one that was all about pleasure.

Instead, he slid his hands from her shoulders, down her arms and held both of her hands. 'I texted you. I called in on the off chance that you'd still be here.'

'Sorry,' she said, squeezing his hands. 'I was in the shower. Everyone else has left for the day.' Her eyes were huge in the gloom, expressive and vulnerable and full of questions. He wanted to chase away every one of her demons. But that was a boundary he had no right in breaching, not when they'd vowed to keep this casual.

She gave him a sexy smile, her tongue touching her bottom lip as she gripped his hands tighter and stepped closer so their bodies were flush.

'What did the text say?' she asked, clearly unwilling to release his hands to check her phone.

He let go of one hand to wrap his arm around her waist and dragged her close. Her pupils dilated. 'I wondered if you would like to go for a drink. I know this lovely pub in Little Dunnop. It's quiet and has a roaring fire.'

Her face fell, a frown settling between her brows.

Aaron swallowed, wondering how he'd ruined the mood. Perhaps she was hesitant to be seen alone with him in public.

'It's a couple of villages away,' he cajoled. 'Hopefully none of my patients will be there, so we're almost guaranteed an evening free of medical drama.'

Her stare rose to his. 'It's not that.' Her teeth scraped her bottom lip, and he instinctively relaxed his hold of her, in case she felt that they were rushing into this.

'It's just that my ex is from Little Dunnop.' She lifted her hand to his chest, her fingers curling into his sweater. 'I don't want to run into him or any of his family.'

Aaron winced, gutted that he hadn't thought of that. 'Of course. I understand. We can go somewhere else.'

'Where's Charlie tonight?' she asked as she looked up at him, her gorgeous eyes pools of desire.

'He's sleeping over at his grandparents' house. They like to take him out on Saturday morning.'

'In that case, no, thanks.' She raised her face,

brushed his lips with hers, barely touching but igniting his nervous system. 'I'll give the pub a miss. Do you have a fire at your place?'

'Mmm-hmm,' he said. 'One to rival any pub's in the county.'

Desperate to ravage those tantalising lips of hers, he held back, loving the direction of this conversation.

'Do you have wine?' she asked, her index finger teasing the stubble along his jaw.

'Yes.'

'A condom machine in the bathroom?' She grinned, and he laughed at her sense of humour.

'Not exactly, but we're covered.' He wrapped both of his arms around her waist, what was left of his restraint vanishing. He hauled her into his arms, crushed her chest to his and slanted his mouth over hers at last.

Stella clung to him, parted her lips and returned his heated kiss as if they'd been kissing for years, as if they were made for kissing and nothing else, as if she'd be happy to spend the night in this very spot that smelled of sweet hay and horseflesh and kiss all night long.

When they parted briefly for air, she moaned, dropping her head back and closing her eyes. 'Invite me back to yours,' she said, her voice slurred with passion. Passion he'd inflamed.

'Whatever you say.' He speared his fingers

through her glossy hair to angle her head so he could taste the soft skin of her neck in an exploratory journey he wanted never to end.

She moaned, her eyes still closed as she slipped her hands under his sweater, her fingers digging into his back, urging his body closer.

Aaron thanked the universe for his smarts; he wasn't stupid enough to question a woman when she issued a direct order. 'Come back to mine.' He held her face, his stare glued to her, felt her small, definite nod.

He made the four-mile drive home in record time.

CHAPTER NINE

THE MINUTE AARON'S front door closed behind them, banishing the November chill from his farmhouse-style cottage, Stella spun to face him. In unison and without a second's hesitation they reached for each other, tugging off each other's coats and hats while indulging in frantic, breathless kisses. Stella had never felt a fire as intense as the one burning her alive, the urgency almost too much to bear.

How could she need him so much?

It was just sex. That was what she recited over and over. They'd agreed: one night.

With a grunt Aaron swung her around and pressed her back up against some piece of furniture in the hallway, his thigh pushing between her legs. She lost herself, her only coherent thought that she would welcome him taking her right here on the flagstone floor.

Aaron tore his lips from hers, his breath gusting as he trailed kisses over her jaw and down her neck. He groaned, his voracious mouth finding every one of her neck's erogenous zones.

'Do you want that drink?' He pulled away, and Stella almost sagged into a heap.

'Later. I want you.' She heeled off her boots, gripped the belt loops on his jeans and tugged his hips between her spread thighs.

He cupped her cheek, and then both cheeks, tilting up her chin to stare down into her eyes. 'You are so beautiful, too good to be true. I plan to distract you with so much pleasure that you won't have a chance to come to your senses.'

'I'm not going anywhere.'

'Lucky me.' Something shifted across his expression—a moment of hesitation, a flash of vulnerability she dared not analyse. 'Can you stay all night?'

'Yes.'

He smiled a dazzling smile that made Stella weak.

She tugged at his waist, bringing his mouth back to hers, until their lips fused, their tongues sweeping to meet and tangle. His fingers curled into her hair and Stella hooked her arms over his wide shoulders, clinging tight.

Aaron hoisted her from the floor. She wrapped her legs around his waist and felt his erection between her legs. He carried her across the room to a wide, comfy sofa in front of the hearth, where the fire had burned low, but still gave off an orange glow and waves of heat. Not that she needed the flames; she was on fire for this man.

Aaron sat on the sofa, lowering Stella into his lap, where she straddled his thighs and stared down at his sincere and hungry expression.

He wanted her. Aaron Bennett thought she was beautiful. This must be a dream.

And tomorrow she would need to wake up. But not yet.

She kissed his jaw, his earlobe, down his neck, as all the while she worked on his shirt buttons. When she parted the soft fabric that smelled like washing powder and Aaron, she caught her bottom lip under her teeth to halt a sigh of utter longing.

He was gorgeous under the clothes, better than she'd imagined. Every muscle of his chest and abdomen was defined. Soft golden hair nestled between his pecs and formed a trail that disappeared beneath the waistband of his jeans.

Stella ran her hands over the warm ridges and dips, learning the feel of him, the places that made his eyes darken like a stormy ocean and his hands restlessly fist her hips. She continued her exploration, and he sighed, his head falling back against the sofa.

'I haven't done this for a while,' he said, his

eyes ablaze with enough desire to assure Stella that he didn't need to worry.

'Me neither.' Stella wasn't sure that she'd ever done whatever *this* was, but she shuddered to think that it would carry that degree of significance. She couldn't allow that. It was just for tonight, except she'd never before felt this all-consuming obsession, this urgent and confusing need to both slowly study every millimetre of Aaron Bennett and to tear at him until he quenched the fire burning her to ash.

She pushed the shirt from his shoulders and popped the button on his jeans, emboldened by the bulge behind his fly. She was no longer the shy, naive Stella that had once lived here. She was Dr Stella Wright, a strong, resilient woman who created her own destiny.

'Who knew you were hiding all of this under those woolly jumpers?' she teased, sitting back on his muscular thighs.

He laughed, reaching for the hem of her own sweater. She raised it over her head, tossing it to the floor.

'The first time I saw you at the hospital when I interviewed for the lecturing post back in the summer, I almost swallowed my tongue.' He slid his warm hands along her ribs and cupped her breasts through her bra. 'You're a striking woman, but the confident way you carry yourself, your fun, self-possessed attitude… I have to admit I was a little in awe of you that day we first spoke.'

In awe of her?

'Why?' She moved her hands over the smooth skin of his shoulders, too desperate to know every inch of him to pause her exploration.

'I was so attracted to you, but figured I was too old, that you would never look at me this way.' He cupped her cheek, his thumb tracing her lips.

'I happen to find your brand of maturity and responsibility a major turn-on,' she said.

Harry had made a big deal of their few-years age gap at the end. She had always suspected that it was a coward's excuse.

A lump she didn't want to acknowledge to-night lodged in her throat. Aaron was so different from Harry. She was different too. No longer young and lovestruck.

Now she could protect herself, keep her emotions distant.

'And I was wildly attracted to you, too,' she confessed. 'I was so busy ogling you, I almost fell down the auditorium steps.'

The look of wonder and desire on his face made her whimper. Emotion she couldn't name bubbled to the surface.

'Now, stop talking,' she mumbled against his

lips. She needed to switch off her thoughts, lose herself in sensation. Tonight belonged to just the two of them, would be their secret to treasure. She'd hold it inside, never tell a soul, relive the memory.

Aaron reached around and popped the clasp of her bra, single-handed. 'Do you want to move upstairs?'

'No. Impressive bra skills, by the way.' Despite the glow of the fire at her back, which bathed Aaron's skin in golden light, Stella's skin pimpled. She wanted to joke, to banter with him to keep things light, but she was already in over her head.

'I still have some moves.' Aaron stroked her back, his fingers lazy and hypnotic where his stare clinging to hers was urgent and voracious.

She nodded, sat up and slipped first one bra strap and then the other from her shoulders and tossed it to the floor. 'Show me,' she said in a breathy voice.

His stare grew intense in that way she'd come to love this week. Every time their eyes met at work, every glance or chance encounter around the health centre, felt deliciously illicit, as if they'd orchestrated a secret rendezvous.

He tugged her waist and she sank into him, their naked torsos burning where they connected. Every inch of his skin was like hot silk. His scent engulfed her until she was certain she'd never eradicate it from her senses. Her head swam with lack of oxygen, but she couldn't tear her mouth away from his wonderful kisses, which were the sweetest, most reckless indulgence she'd ever experienced.

Only she wanted more. She wanted everything he'd give her, for one night. Then she could leave Abbotsford once more knowing that she hadn't been controlled by her fears, that he'd been right: she could be herself anywhere she chose.

His warm palms cupped her breasts, and Stella dropped her head back on a moan as he thumbed both of her nipples. Her hips rocked of their own accord, seeking out friction to help her weather the storm tossing her body. When Aaron's mouth closed over one nipple, she cried out and tangled her fingers in his hair. Nothing mattered but this one precious night. Her fears, her doubts, their pasts, and futures…all irrelevant.

Stella was vaguely aware of the removal of their remaining clothes, her attention too focused on how Aaron made her feel invincible and beautiful and desired to care about the scramble of limbs and tangle of clothes. She watched him take a condom from his wallet and cover himself, her desperation reaching dizzying heights. And then he was pushing inside her, his eyes locked with hers, his hands cupping her face as if she were a prized possession, and for all she knew the sky might be falling down.

'Stella,' he muttered, the desire in his eyes scorching her skin.

She clung to him, surrounded by his strong arms. She lost herself in returning his every kiss. When he retreated, she surged to meet him. When he gripped her hands, his fingers laced with hers, she clung tighter, surrounded his hips with her legs. When she moaned his name, he urged her on, muttering her name into her hair, the crook of her neck, her ear, his warm breath dancing over her sensitised skin, adding a cascade of shivers to the rapture already taking hold. She shattered, his name on her broken cry, her climax powerful and endless.

Aaron collapsed his weight on top of her with a groan, joining her in bliss, and Stella entered a world where reality exceeded fantasy. A world where she knew exactly what it felt like to be with Aaron Bennett.

A world that she feared was changed for ever.

Aaron drowsily stroked the length of Stella's arm, which was warm from the fire's glow where he'd banked it with fresh logs. They occupied the sofa, their limbs entwined, a blanket covering them. He wove his fingers with hers, unable to stop touching her for even a second. A fleeting rush of panic stalled his breath. What if he couldn't ever stop?

No, they'd agreed on one night. They had hours until dawn, hours until he would shrug off the role of lover he'd donned for the night and resume the most important role of his life: that of Charlie's father.

Only now that he'd met Stella, now that they had crossed that line of physical intimacy, the constant guilt he'd lived with since Molly's death roared back to life, louder than ever.

He swallowed, fighting the urge to take Stella home and retreat into himself. How could he enjoy being with her when he carried so much baggage that made him feel unworthy? There was no need to fear that he was already addicted to Stella. He couldn't allow himself such an amazing privilege. He'd had his chance at love. That was why this one night of passion was all he could justify, all he could permit.

He shifted, tightening his grip on her waist, and asked in a low voice, 'Tell me what happened to turn you against Abbotsford?' It was obviously linked to this no-good ex, the one who'd cruelly used her, lied and then cast her aside. He hated that she denied herself the place she'd grown up.

He expected her small sigh, so he feathered his lips over her bare shoulder in light kisses, letting her know that nothing she told him would matter or alter how he felt about her.

His stomach rolled at the depth of those feelings he had no right to feel. But he could push those down. He would have to. For Stella, for Charlie and for his own sanity.

She turned onto her back, her head resting on his bicep, where she was still tucked into the crook of his arm. He stroked her hair back from her face and kissed her warm cheek.

'It wasn't Abbotsford as such, just the close-knit nature of village life. Everyone knowing your business.' She sighed and Aaron pressed his lips to her temple, willing her to open up. Perhaps he could reassure her that whatever she feared no longer carried the threat she perceived.

'My break-up with Harry was all such a mess at the time. I didn't know until he texted to break things off, but he didn't stop sleeping with his ex, Angus's mum, throughout our entire relationship.'

Aaron stiffened, protective urges welling up inside him. 'He strung you along and broke up with you in a text?'

She nodded, dragging in a fortifying breath, but he saw the pain still there beneath the surface. 'I believed him when he said he loved me,' she whispered. 'He was older than me, more experienced. He was my first, you know. I trusted him.'

Aaron's muscles coiled tight with rage. 'And he betrayed all of that, after he'd allowed you to get close to his son, to care about them both.' How could someone be such a snake? How could he use a person with such a big heart as Stella? She deserved so much better.

'I was so humiliated,' she continued. 'One minute he was professing undying love and including me in his and Angus's daily lives, then all of a sudden he said it was over, that he was going back to his ex. He even had the audacity to say it was for Angus's sake. And I, in my naiveté, believed him. It wasn't until later that I realised Harry always did what was best for Harry.'

Aaron bit his lip to stop himself from asking for more details. Her pain was a gnawing rumble in his gut. But there must be more to the story for her to avoid Abbotsford, avoid people who might have known her back then.

'Then the rumours started,' she said in a whisper he might not have heard if he hadn't been so close.

He froze, his breath stalling. 'What rumours?'

'Mum came home from work one day upset. People were saying that I'd been the reason Harry and his ex had split in the first place. That I was the other woman, the kind of person who thought I could break up a lovely young family for my own selfish reasons.'

'But it wasn't true.' He knew deep down in his bones that she was incapable of selfishness.

She shook her head, but she wouldn't look at him. 'I didn't know about Angus's mother. He told me he was single. He swept me off my feet. When he confessed that he had a son with a shared custody arrangement, I was delighted, already besotted and half in love with him. I was young, stupid. I should have seen through him, realised the spin was too good to be true.'

Outraged on her behalf, Aaron snorted. 'You were young. That doesn't mean you deserved to be treated that way, that you should have been able to read his mind, or that you were in any way responsible for *his* actions.'

She nodded, her eyes sadder than ever. 'I can certainly understand that now, but at the time none of it mattered. I was lost in my grief, crying all the time. Initially I was too heartbroken to care what people thought. I missed Angus. I grieved the loss of both relationships. And then later I became paranoid and anxious, refusing to leave the house in case someone said something to me and I'd break down in the street.'

'And this… Harry. Didn't he deny the rumours, defend you, tell the truth?' What kind of a man would stand by and let an innocent woman he must have cared for a little suffer alone?

'No. That was the most humiliating part of all.

It was as if he'd vanished, leaving me to clean up his dirty work.'

He rested his forehead against her temple, breathed in her warm scent. 'I know it would have been cold comfort at the time, but you must know that he never deserved you.'

Could she possibly still be in love with this guy?

Nausea gripped his throat.

She shrugged. 'I know that now. But then I wondered if his ex was responsible for starting the rumours. Or maybe Harry himself to garner sympathy and win her back for good. I don't know. The worst part was that I was so blind to what I thought love was that I truly believed we had a future. That I would go to uni but come home every weekend to be with him and Angus. That one day I'd move back here and we would be a proper family. More fool me.'

'It wasn't your fault.' He stroked her hair, knowing that he'd lost her to her memories of the pain she'd suffered.

'They were already a family,' she continued as if she hadn't heard, 'one that didn't include me.' She met his eyes. 'I was just a discarded side-piece.'

Aaron bit back a litany of curses, seeing red on Stella's behalf. 'I'm sorry that you had that experience, that this Harry guy was too much of a coward to be honest. That he behaved so cruelly.'

She shrugged but he knew a brave face when he saw one. 'It worked out for the best. I was leaving for uni anyway. When I got to London, I kept busy as a distraction, threw myself into being a medical student, worked hard and played hard.'

She smiled her wide smile and winked at him. 'I had a blast, swapped horses for parties and clubbing during any spare time I had. London is good like that—diverting, energetic, always abuzz. Pretty soon I was too busy to even think about Harry.'

'But it stopped you visiting home.' She hadn't dated again. She wasn't over it.

Acid burned behind his sternum.

She shrugged, still holding part of herself aloof, still shielding. 'You know how demanding those years are academically. I spent most of my free time studying, with the occasional party thrown in. Plus my parents often visited London, as all three of their daughters were based there. In fact, they often talk about selling up here and relocating. I suspect they will once either of my sisters starts a family.'

Aaron's heart skipped a beat without reason. 'What about you? Don't you want children one day?' It was none of his business and he shouldn't be invested in her answer. But he cared about her. He wanted her to be happy and fulfilled.

She shook her head. 'It's not something I've really considered, probably because I haven't had a serious relationship since. I love my job. I'm still focused on my career. You know what that's like.'

Silence settled in the room, broken only by the occasional crackle from the fire. Aaron grew inexplicably restless. It shouldn't matter to him that she had no plans to settle down. But he felt as if he'd just been handed a million-pound note, only to discover it was fake.

'What about you?' she said, deflecting the heat away from herself. 'Have you thought about moving on? Getting married again?' She turned onto her stomach, dipped her gaze and toyed with his chest hair, as if she cared about his future happiness. But she was just being thoughtful. She'd just confessed her reasons to fear falling in love again. She only wanted a one-night stand and she still planned to move away, despite her success at the practice.

And her practicality suited him down to the ground. Right...?

'Not really.' Aaron stroked her back, forced his body to relax, because he did care that they had this connection she could clearly take or leave, even though he shouldn't. 'Life is so busy. Charlie takes up all of my free time. I can't imagine there would be too many women willing to settle for the very occasional date sandwiched in between school pick-up and bedtime stories.'

He felt the same as her about relationships, so why was he so…irritated to hear her voice that her intentions hadn't changed just because they'd had amazing sex?

She stroked his hair, her eyes heavy. 'I think you'd be surprised when you do decide to dip your toe back into the dating pool. I witnessed quite the hormonal kerfuffle at the school gate last week. I suspect the single ladies would be lining up to date the Cotswolds' most eligible doctor.'

He laughed at the picture she painted, but the idea made Aaron shudder. Until she'd returned to Abbotsford, he'd had no interest in the local women, in women full stop.

'I can't do it to Charlie,' he said, the old guilt crawling under his skin. 'He needs me at the moment, needs all of my attention. I have to be everything to him, Mum and Dad.'

She seemed taken aback. 'So that's it for you dating-wise? Your personal needs are irrelevant because you became a parent?'

There was no accusation in her tone, just pensive curiosity.

He shrugged, because he'd never actually

given it this much consideration. 'Maybe when he's older I'll have time to date.'

But Charlie wasn't the main reason that he kept himself emotionally unavailable. He couldn't trust that he wouldn't let someone he cared for down again in the future, that he would have to relive the pain of loss. He'd rather be alone.

'How old,' she asked, 'like eighteen? When he leaves for uni?' She chuckled softly but there was something watchful, searching in her eyes.

Why was she so interested in his dating life? Had she changed her mind about the one-night rule? Perhaps his moves weren't that rusty.

His silence was the only answer he had. He couldn't seriously contemplate inviting another woman into his and Charlie's life. What if his son formed an attachment and the relationship didn't last? Look at the way Stella had been hurt. Like her, he couldn't bear to think of poor, confused baby Angus. What if a new woman in Aaron's life resurrected all of Charlie's questions about his mother's death, issues he'd dealt with? What if he grew up to resent Aaron for his choice to move on?

He'd never do anything to risk losing his son. He didn't want Molly's death to mean nothing.

At his continued stillness, Stella stroked his cheek. 'I understand. You're the most important person in Charlie's life. Of course you want to protect him. That's as it should be.' She pressed her mouth to his, comprehension in her eyes.

Because she did understand. She'd been on the receiving end of the choices some parents made to put their own, often messed up and selfish feelings first, and she'd been hurt in the crossfire.

But right now, still rocked by their chemistry and the intimacy of having her naked in his arms, Aaron's predominant fear was for himself, for his precious status quo.

Rather than examine his feelings further, he ran with her kiss, turning it from something comforting to something carnal, his body reacting to hers, his mind forgetting all of the reasons this couldn't last beyond tonight as he covered her body with his. They still had a few hours before sunrise. The best way to combat his concerns, to forget why he couldn't date, why Stella, who shared his reservations, was perfect for now?

The distraction of pleasure.

CHAPTER TEN

BY THE END of a busy Wednesday the following week, Stella was enjoying an erotic daydream of Aaron as she had filled every spare moment since her amazing night his bed.

The door swung open, startling her from the emails she had read and reread at least six times. She looked up from the computer, her heart lurching with predictable arousal and excitement at the sight of Aaron.

One look at his serious expression dissolved her desire, her stomach pinching with trepidation.

'There's an emergency on Penwood Hill,' he said of the local beauty spot popular with hikers. 'Community First Responders have been called, but I'm going to assist in case they need help.'

Stella stood, adrenaline shoving her body into action. 'Can I come, too?'

Aaron nodded, his eyes, which carried the glimmer of intimacy, holding hers. 'I hoped you'd want to. Let's go.'

In Stella's mind, a hundred silent communications seemed to pass between them, things they couldn't voice aloud right now, maybe never.

Do you regret what we did?

Have you thought about me since?

Are you, like me, desperate to do it again?

But now was not the time to have any of those conversations and who knew what Aaron was thinking?

As they exited her consultation room, Aaron reached for her hand. A thrill coursed through her at his simple touch, one that had nothing to do with the adrenaline of attending a medical emergency out in the field. This rush was all about the way Aaron didn't seem to care who saw them holding hands as he led her through the surgery where staff were finishing up for the day and the last patient lingered, chatting about his arthritic knee.

Stella tried to breathe through the sensation that people were staring, judging her, gossiping. It was likely all in her head. But she didn't want the locals to think she was making a play for the village's most eligible man.

Perhaps Aaron had acted unconsciously. She should have eased her hand away—the physical side of their relationship was meant to be over. Except the last time she had felt absolutely comfortable holding a man's hand—something she didn't do when she dated casually—was with Harry.

But there was no time to overthink the gesture, or interpret it as the kind of emotional entanglement that she normally avoided. In the utility room at the rear of the practice, Aaron grabbed two high-visibility all-weather jackets from the hooks on the wall and headed out to the car park with Stella in tow.

They climbed into a four-wheel drive emblazoned with the words 'Abbotsford Medical Centre', and Aaron punched an address into the vehicle's GPS.

'Tell me what we're dealing with,' said Stella, focused on the scene they would find as she clicked her seatbelt into place.

'A day tourist has slipped and fallen running the Penwood Track. Possible tib and fib fracture.' Aaron navigated the car from the car park behind the surgery and took a left turn in the direction of the neighbouring village of Penwood.

He glanced her way, his calm-under-pressure confidence as reassuring as his open smile. 'It's complicated by the fact that his wife, who is thirty-six weeks pregnant, was waiting for him in the car. By all accounts, she tried to help him down the track, but started to have strong contractions.'

'So a double emergency?' Stella's mind raced,

running through a plan to triage both patients as soon as they reached the scene.

He nodded, his eyes narrowed with urgency. 'Don't worry.' He reached across the central console and squeezed her hand. 'We can do this. The car is equipped with everything we might need.'

At Stella's hesitant nod, he continued. 'The wife became concerned when he didn't come back from his run—he's a fell runner—within his expected time. There's no mobile reception on the track, so she rushed back to the car to sound the alarm.'

He exhaled a controlled breath, a small smile just for her on his lips. 'I told you—never a dull moment around here.'

They shared a second's eye contact that had Stella recalling every touch, every kiss, every cry of their passionate night together.

Face flushed from the erotic memories, she glanced over her shoulder to the well-stocked boot while Aaron focused on the road.

'Do we have Entonox?' she asked.

'Yes. And the community responder is there, but it's his first week without supervision, poor guy.'

Pulse racing, Stella recognised the route Aaron was taking.

'You're not going to follow the road, are you?'

she asked as they bumped over a pothole at speed, flicking up gravel.

'Yes. This is the quickest route to Penwood.' He glanced at the GPS, which wouldn't know the short cut over private land that Stella knew like the back of her hand.

She shook her head. 'No, don't go through the village. The fastest way to the start of the Penwood Track is through the Brady farm, you know, Dale Brady's land.'

'Are you sure?' He shot her a searching look before taking a bend in the lane.

'Absolutely. I used to ride that way all the time on Gertrude. The farm track is wide enough for a four-wheel drive and it cuts off the corner taken via the road. Trust me. It's quicker.'

Aaron grinned and then winked. 'Whatever you say. I do trust you. Nothing much changes around this landscape. You probably know the area better than me, as I was more about driving flashy sports cars around Cheltenham than I was about taking a horse or a Land Rover over a farm track in my youth.'

Stella pursed her lips. 'Oh, I recall. You always seemed to have a different pretty female passenger, too.'

He grinned, the moment of lightness punctuating the adrenaline rush seemingly as welcome to him as it was to Stella. He reached for her hand once more, raising it to his mouth to press a kiss across her knuckles. 'Thank you for the insider knowledge. I'm glad that you're here.'

His smile, the touch of his lips to her skin, devastated Stella, who had managed to fool herself that she could move on from their one night, but she'd been sorely deluded. Not that there was time to enjoy the shudders his touch sent through her body, or panic at her realisation that she was in deep trouble where Aaron was concerned.

He was everything she had avoided these past nine years: perfect, a man made just for Stella.

She stared out of the window to stop herself staring at him. Of course he wasn't perfect. No one was. He had as many issues, as many reasons to avoid a serious relationship as she did. She just couldn't decide if that gave her solace or left a sour taste in her mouth.

At Stella's direction, Aaron took a right turn and headed for the Brady farm.

Stella pointed out the dirt road, her stomach now churning with more than adrenaline for the medical scene awaiting them as she replayed their conversation. Aaron was right. In many ways, she too was a local. She'd grown up here, had family here, was a part of local hIstory.

A sharp pain lodged under her ribs. She hadn't realised how much she was enjoying being back in her old stomping ground. How much she'd missed riding and walking this landscape. She had been forced to become another version of herself in this place, one she didn't like: gullible, broken, grieving. Her desire to leave Abbotsford and return to London had nothing to do with the place and everything to do with her aversion to being hurt again. But seeing the village, the people, the community through Aaron's eyes, she realised that the association between place and her past that she'd made was a figment of her imagination. An unhealthy link that kept her bound in fear.

That just wouldn't do.

Before Stella could ponder this momentous realisation, they arrived at the start of the Penwood Track. The single-lane road flared into a small turning circle, which doubled as a makeshift car park for those wanting to hike the track.

Aaron pulled up behind the first responder's vehicle, which was parked next to the only other car. A heavily pregnant woman was leaning against the car, one hand braced on the open driver's side door and the other on the roof of the car.

Aaron had barely engaged the handbrake when Stella flung open the passenger door and ran towards the woman. She was clearly in the middle of a strong contraction, breathing hard through the pain but in a controlled way that told Stella she'd likely laboured before.

Aaron joined them a few seconds later, one medical backpack slung over his shoulder and another which he placed on the ground at Stella's feet. 'I'll go and assist the first responder, who is with the husband. I'll do a quick triage and then I'll come back, okay?'

Stella nodded, wishing they could stick together.

Aaron addressed the woman. 'Don't worry, Mrs Heath, the ambulance is on its way.'

Then he handed Stella a head torch and took the track at a run, disappearing from sight around the bend.

As the woman's contraction passed, Stella rested a hand on her arm. 'My name is Stella, I'm a GP from Abbotsford.' She ignored how naturally that sentence formed. 'What's your first name, Mrs Heath?'

'Abby,' the woman said, gripping Stella's hand with determination bordering on panic.

This wasn't good. Stella needed to transport Abby somewhere suitable, comfortable and clean. But she had seen that look before during her obstetric post, often when a woman was transitioning into the second stage of labour.

'Can you walk?' Stella asked, glancing over

her shoulder to where the practice vehicle was parked only five metres away.

Abby shook her head, her hand gripping Stella's in a vice, her breathing becoming deep and deliberate once more. 'Need to push,' she said, scrunching her eyes closed against the pain of another powerful contraction.

Stella soothed the woman through the worst of it, her mind spinning. Her gaze searched the track for Aaron, but of course he hadn't had enough time to find the husband, let alone return to assist Stella. She had never delivered a baby outside of a hospital before. But nature waited for no one. If baby Heath was on its way, she would have to manage with what they had to hand.

'Could you move into the back of your car?'

At Abby's uncertain nod, Stella guided her the couple of steps, opened the rear door of the car and helped lower her into a sitting position on the edge of the back seat.

Stella rummaged in the backpack, finding all of the basics, but if the baby came before the ambulance arrived she would need to be prepared.

'I need to get some more supplies,' she said to Abby. 'I have gas and air in the car. I'll be thirty seconds, okay?'

Abby nodded and Stella rushed to the four-wheel drive and flung open the boot, scooping up an armful of blankets and a cannister of Entonox. She returned to Abby, her training kicking in, using but also mitigating her own flight response.

She could do this, alone if she had to. She could help Abby. She could make a difference here. That was why she had wanted to be a GP.

As she searched the contents of the bag in the light from the torch, part of her wanted to laugh at how she'd once foolishly thought working in Abbotsford would be a dull, uneventful, snooze fest. But that had been her fear talking. Another lie she'd believed to protect herself from being as vulnerable as she had once been when she was eighteen.

'I need to push,' said Abby, gripping the driver's headrest with white-knuckle force.

Stella nodded calmly, managed a smile and saw its immediate effect on Abby's wild eyes.

She removed the packaging from a plastic mouthpiece. 'Is this your first baby?' Stella connected the mouthpiece to the cannister of Entonox.

Abby took the mouthpiece from Stella and began sucking on it as another contraction took hold.

'Second,' said Abby when she could next speak. 'The baby's coming. I can't hold on.'

'Okay. It's going to be fine.' Stella pulled on a pair of latex gloves, wishing that she had Aaron's calming presence but also confident that she had been trained for this.

'You and I are going to do this together, okay?' Stella spread a blanket under Abby's legs and another around her shoulders to ward off the cold the dusk brought. Then she eased Abby's clothing down, covering her lap with a clean towel.

'I need to examine you quickly, just to make sure the baby is head first. We'll wait until the next contraction, and I'll be as gentle as I can.'

Abby nodded, her nostrils flaring as a fresh contraction started. Stella quickly established that Abby was fully dilated and indeed in full-blown second-stage labour.

'I can feel your baby's head, Abby. Everything looks great. Are you having a boy or a girl?' She changed her gloves.

'Boy,' Abby panted.

Then there was the scrunch of gravel and an out-of-breath Aaron arrived. Stella all but sagged with relief.

With an expert eye, he took in the scene and, as Abby's contraction passed and she stopped pushing, joined them in the small space the open car door allowed.

'This is Abby and she's having a baby boy,' Stella said, grateful that they'd have the benefit of Aaron's experience and an extra pair of hands.

'Abby, I'm Dr Bennett. I've just examined your

husband and he's going to be absolutely fine. He has broken his leg, but I gave him some pain medication and he's warm and comfortable and stable. You don't need to worry about him, okay? He said he loves you and he's going to be with you as soon as help arrives to carry him down the hill.'

'The baby isn't far away,' Stella informed Aaron. 'I've checked and he's a cephalic presentation.'

'Good, well done.' Aaron reached for a pair of gloves, his stare locking with Stella's. She saw his own trace of trepidation. Like her, he was probably thinking of all the things that could go wrong with baby Heath's delivery. Was he also recalling the birth of his own son, the wonderful, much anticipated moment that had rapidly turned to every husband's worst nightmare?

She wanted to hold him, to match their physical closeness to the emotional connection she could no longer deny existed. She wanted to press her lips to the fine frown lines in the corners of his eyes until she had magically chased away any residue of his pain. Instead she smiled, hoping he could read reassurance and togetherness in her eyes in the same way she saw it beaming from his.

'We can do this,' he said, his smile stretching

for Stella, and then to Abby said, 'Everything is going to be fine.'

Stella nodded in agreement and returned all her attention to Abby.

Over the next ten minutes the three of them worked as a team, their mutual trust and respect helping ease baby boy Heath into the world. There were tears from both women as Stella placed the tiny newborn in his mother's arms for the first time.

When Stella turned her relieved smile on Aaron she saw that he too was misty-eyed.

Then tears turned to delighted laughter as Aaron and Stella hugged awkwardly over the medical paraphernalia littering the ground. Stella clung to him, breathed in his familiar scent, revelled in the masculine strength of his body, her euphoria latching on to Aaron and their growing bond.

When she pulled away to check on Abby and the baby, out of nowhere chills of doubt attacked her body. Aaron had already experienced all of this with Molly. Aaron had Charlie and wasn't looking for a relationship.

More reconciled than ever that they were right to give their fling a one-night limit, she shakily packed away the equipment, avoiding glancing at Aaron.

In the next few minutes two ambulances arrived, each unloading a stretcher. Stella shoved away her conflicting emotions—fear that she'd begun to feel closer to Aaron than was wise, and relief that she'd held something back—and helped the paramedics to load Abby and the baby into the back of the ambulance. Once connected to an oxygen saturation monitor, the baby was deemed fine and healthy.

Mr Heath was carried down the hill and placed in the second ambulance, but not before more tears all round as he was introduced to his tiny son.

The minute both ambulances headed back towards Cheltenham, Stella's arms sagged to her sides, the adrenaline that had served her well draining away to nothing. It wasn't until she was seated once more in the passenger seat of the practice four-wheel drive that the tremors began.

'That was incredible,' she said, the memory of the tiny, precious newborn's weight in her arms still fresh.

She glanced at his profile, searching for the impossible, for something she feared and craved simultaneously: that his feelings resembled hers.

All she saw were shadows.

'Thank you.' Her voice broke and her eyes burned, her jumbled emotions expanding.

Had Aaron experienced the wonder she saw on the Heaths' faces when he'd first held Charlie? How quickly had that wonder turned to horror for his wife, and how could he ever get over such a monumental loss?

'What for?' Aaron gripped her hand across the centre console and squeezed. 'You and Abby did all of the work. I'm so proud of you.'

His eyes were haunted. Stella knew him well enough to see his flicker of pain, and she couldn't help the urge to offer comfort, to gently probe and ensure the delivery hadn't brought back bittersweet memories of Charlie's birth and the subsequent trauma of Molly's death.

'Can you pull over?' Stella managed to choke out.

He did so without question, perhaps sensing the unforeseen seismic shift happening inside Stella. Her head labelled it an anticlimax, but her heart perceived a sledgehammer blow of realisation.

Her self-preservation refused to label her feelings. But watching the love and connection of the Heath family and feeling the profound connection to Aaron that went way beyond physical attraction, she knew that she wanted that for herself one day. A partner so in sync with her that they could communicate with their eyes and their smiles alone. A baby that she made with the love of her life. All these years she had told herself that she had the life she wanted, but it had all been lies. She'd been hiding, pretending that she was complete so she could armour her heart.

But sharing that experience with Aaron made her aware just how much she was short-changing herself in life, denying herself its most wondrous experiences: deep love, sharing her life with someone, creating a family of their own with that person.

Aaron turned off the engine and the car filled with silence.

She unclipped her seatbelt and turned to face him, almost deaf from the thundering of her heart. 'Are...are *you* okay?'

The sadness in his expression as he registered the unspoken question behind her question tore through her chest.

She asked it anyway, because she wanted to be there for him. 'Did it bring back memories... of Charlie's birth?'

He swallowed, his gaze shifting. 'A little. I'm just so relieved that they were both okay.' He stared out through the windscreen. Darkness had descended, giving the impression that they were wrapped in their own warm, safe cocoon.

But she couldn't trust impressions.

She ached for Aaron's loss, but at the same time crumpled a little for herself. The irony of her perfect man being in love with someone else, someone ethereal and intangible, someone Stella could never rival, roared in her head, a feral scream of the danger of letting down her guard.

As Aaron stayed silent, Stella switched subjects.

'I want to thank you for everything,' she said, a lump of longing in her throat. 'For bringing me along today. For inviting me to your practice in the first place.' She looked at her hands in her lap. 'I never said thank you for taking me on, even when I disparaged your home, your workplace, your life. But I appreciate everything you've done for me. I appreciate all the opportunities you've given me.'

I appreciate you.

Too close to tears, she couldn't bring herself to utter the last sentiment aloud. She might hurl herself into his arms in search of the heady rush and rightness she knew that she would find there.

'You're welcome.' He tilted his head and seemed to see into her soul. 'Thank *you* for suggesting that short cut and for being your wonderful self back there.' He brushed some hair back from her face. His pupils were wide, swallowing the blue she loved. 'Inviting you here was one of my smarter moves.'

'I'm glad that you did.'

'It's rewarding, isn't it? Making a difference.'

He cupped her cheek, soothing some of the turmoil she carried. 'That's what I love about this job.'

She nodded, frozen by her needs. It had been years since she'd felt a true part of this community. Aaron's patience and persistence had shown her that she could be herself, no matter where she was and be valued, be a part of something bigger than herself. That she mattered, despite the memories tangled up with this place.

And now, for the first time in years, she wanted that in her personal life as well as professionally.

They stared at each other for a handful of heartbeats.

His eyes swooped to her mouth. Tension resonated from him; he was holding back, perhaps both words and actions.

Before she could question the impulse, Stella scrambled into his lap, her knees astride his thighs, and threw her arms around his neck. She couldn't deny her feelings, which hadn't lessened despite their one night as lovers.

She craved him more than ever.

Aaron's hand settled warm and comforting in the middle of her back, his stare dark, vulnerable.

Tired of restraint, she pressed her mouth to his in a cathartic surrender. He returned her kiss with a groan of release, as if he too had held back for too long.

They had broken the rules, which, for Stella, somehow sweetened the addictive kisses.

Aaron's hand curled around the back of her neck, holding her mouth in place as she tangled her fingers into his hair, tilted his head back against the headrest. He gripped her waist, fisting her skirt as she rode his lap. His hardness pressed between her legs as he tilted his hips.

Would anything extinguish this fire scorching her alive?

'What are we doing?' he asked as she let him up for air, even as his fingers slid under the hem of her sweater to the naked skin of her back, restlessly flexing, stroking, exploring.

'I don't know.' She feathered kisses over the side of his neck so the warm scent of his body filled her nostrils from inside his collar. She couldn't make her lips leave his skin. 'Perhaps it's just the adrenaline.'

She gripped his face and stared into his eyes. 'I want you.' Over and over until she'd burned him out of her system.

He searched her stare, his eyes transparent, showing her the same needs that paralysed her. 'Me too. Ever since I woke up on Saturday morning to find you gone. I couldn't wait for the start of a new week just to see you.'

His words were beyond worrisome to the part of herself she still needed to protect, but she became distracted by pleasure as his hands skated her sides, cupped her breasts, zapping her nervous system with sparks that felt way too good to be wrong.

'This is bad,' she said as he released her from another soul-searing kiss.

'I know.' He shifted under her, his lips stretching into that sexy smile she'd come to adore. 'Which is probably why it feels so fantastic.'

She writhed in his lap, torturing them both with the friction. 'Like a compulsion. But one night was supposed to be enough.'

Perhaps her addiction, her weakness for him, was amplified because she couldn't walk away yet. Nothing else had changed. Her one relationship had ended in enough desolation to keep her single for nine years, and Aaron was still in love with his wife and devoted only to his son.

He smiled, the playful delight in his eyes lightening the mood. 'So I'm a compulsion now? That's a big step up from a crush.'

Stella rolled her eyes, laughter bubbling up from her chest.

Then he sobered, pressed his forehead to hers and exhaled his frustration. 'I have to go—I need to pick up Charlie.'

As if doused in icy water, Stella pulled away.

She'd become so carried away by her feelings for him, feelings that she'd vowed she could keep in check, that she'd forgotten his personal obligations.

'Of course.' Mortified, she shifted her weight from his thighs, preparing to retake the passenger seat.

'Wait.' He gripped her hips, stared up at her in heartfelt appeal. 'Can we see each other again? Outside of work?' He smiled, cajoling, his eyes vulnerable and hopeful, and Stella wanted to give him anything. Everything.

She swallowed hard, her throat tight with the ache to say *yes*. But, as he'd just reminded her, Aaron and Charlie were a father-and-son team.

No, Aaron wasn't Harry and Stella was no longer trusting and guileless. But normally, by this stage in a relationship—where things moved from casual towards expectant, attached, romantic—she made her excuses and called it a day.

Before she could become emotionally invested.

Perhaps it was already too late.

'Don't you have Charlie to think about?' She needed to remind herself that Aaron was a package deal, that he would always put Charlie first, and that was a good thing. Given that she had just proved that Aaron alone was temptation enough, there was no way she could risk interacting with

Charlie, who, as his father's son, was no doubt equally enchanting. Not if she hoped to keep herself distant enough so she could walk away when the time came.

He nodded, his lips pressed into a flat line. 'Yes.' Regret and realisation that she was right dawned in his eyes.

She reluctantly slid into the passenger seat. 'Let's go back to Abbotsford. It's been a long day.'

He nodded, started the car without comment and drove the four miles in silence. After all, what else was there to say?

CHAPTER ELEVEN

AARON KNEW THE invitation was unwise even as the eager words left his mouth. 'Would you like to join us for dinner?'

He and Charlie had bumped into Stella at the village shop and, try as he might, he couldn't stop himself. She carried a solitary bottle of wine and they hadn't had a moment alone together since he dropped her at home after they had delivered the Heath baby three days ago and kissed in the driver's seat like horny teenagers.

'We're having meatballs and spaghetti.' Charlie beamed, as if the menu might sway her decision. 'It's my favourite. But Dad forgot to buy the pasta sauce, didn't you, Dad?'

'I did.' Aaron met Stella's stare. He was so conflicted that he almost withdrew the invitation. But the deed was done. Charlie had recognised Stella the minute they'd walked into the tiny shop and it was only one home-cooked meal, hardly a grand seduction. It couldn't even really be called a date.

'Um…' She smiled down at Charlie. 'Do you have enough? I don't want to deprive you of your favourite meal.'

'We have lots,' Charlie said dramatically, 'but I'm only allowed three meatballs, because they are this big.' He made a circle with his thumb and forefinger and looked to Aaron for confirmation.

'We normally have leftovers, but it's no big deal,' Aaron eyed her bottle of wine, 'if you have plans.' None of his business.

Stella flushed. 'My parents are out tonight. I was going to have a glass of this and maybe make some cheese on toast.' She shrugged. 'Actually, I'd love to join you for spaghetti, now that you have the sauce.'

They shared another look that made Aaron think they were both wary of the dynamics and of sharing too much. Was Stella, like him, also running out of resolve against the temptation?

Aaron's cottage was a three-minute walk, door-to-door from the shop. Aaron quickly completed the partially prepared meal with the addition of pasta sauce, Charlie set another place at the table for Stella and she poured two glasses of wine.

'See,' said Charlie, pointing with his fork, 'I have three meatballs, and you have three meatballs.' He offered Stella his happy smile as he showed off his maths skills. 'That makes six. It's a double.'

Stella gave Charlie a high five and an impressed nod. 'You're a very smart young man.'

Aaron's heart swelled with pride as he watched Stella interact with Charlie, even as the instant and easy connection between them caused a lump to press against his lungs and restrict his breath. Just like all the other wonderful things he had learned about her, he immediately knew she would make an amazing mother if she ever chose to have children.

He had an urgent and visceral urge to lean across the table and kiss her. In fact, he hadn't stopped wanting to kiss her since that very first time their lips met.

He was so doomed...

She had been right. Delivering the Heath baby with Stella had brought up a sickening collision of his past and present. The wonder of holding his son. The love he'd felt watching Molly kiss his downy head. Then the shock and desolation of his wife, Charlie's mother, being snatched away from them both.

When Abby's baby had been safely delivered he'd clung to Stella in that moment of shared joy, wondering how he had become so desperate for her in such a short space of time.

Watching her now with his son, the answer was obvious. How could he not be utterly captivated?

'What's your favourite part of school?' she asked Charlie.

Aaron stifled a laugh, knowing exactly what his son's response would be. He often asked him that very question and usually received the same answer: lunchtime, with home time in second place.

'I like lunchtime,' said Charlie, predictably. 'Today we had veggie pizza.' He stabbed at a meatball with his fork and waggled it around like a cheerleader's pompom, his 'z's lisped adorably since he had lost his first baby tooth last week.

'Yummy—I like pizza too,' said Stella, catching Aaron's eye once more.

Acknowledgement and communication passed silently between them, as if they had been together for years and knew how the other thought.

In his fantasy, he imagined it went something like:

Stella: *Your son is adorable.*

Aaron: *You're so good with him.*

Both in unison: *It makes me want you all the more.*

But the tightening in his gut reminded him to slow down his wild imaginings. Something out of his control was happening. That he craved her company, her smiles, her sharp wit was un-derstandable. The physical compulsions made sense. But this new longing—that the affinity they had for each other extended to Charlie in Stella's case—mystified him.

He was on dangerous ground, craving the cerebral connection as much as the physical, because Stella might have been specifically de-signed to his specifications.

Only she couldn't be his, just as he wasn't the man for her, neither of them wanting the emo-tional attachment that sometimes felt as if it was developing without their permission.

Aaron filled his mouth with food, giving him-self more time to think. Except he was too out of practice to untangle his emotions, having spent years merely accepting the guilt he lived with and embracing his position.

'Pizza is my favourite,' continued Charlie, oblivious to the adult tension stealing Aaron's appetite and the fact that only half an hour ago he'd declared the same was true for meatballs and spaghetti. 'But Dad always makes the edges too brown and crispy.' His son offered a wither-ing look that spoke of his long suffering under his father's culinary challenges. 'Johnny's mum makes nice, soft edges, like the pizza at school.'

Stella looked away from a sombre Charlie and

pressed her lips together, Aaron assumed to hold in a smile.

'Does he?' She flicked a knowing look at Aaron. 'That's not good. But I have an idea. You could help him by setting a timer on his phone that will tell him when the pizza is ready to come out of the oven. I'll show you how to do it after we eat our meatballs if you like.'

Charlie's eyes went wide, impressed, no doubt delighted that he'd have access to Aaron's phone. Like most parents Aaron constantly struggled to police screen time, but this was a practical, even educational skill, so he could hardly object.

His son's face lit up, his dreamy gaze falling on Stella in a way that meant Aaron would likely be peppered with Stella-related questions for the rest of the week.

Aaron mouthed *Thank you* to Stella and gripped his silverware tighter, fresh guilt tightening his shoulders. For everyone's sake, he couldn't let them become too close. Because Charlie had naturally warmed to Stella, as if his life lacked the influence of a sage and wise woman, even if it was simply to ward off burnt pizza in the future.

The sigh Aaron held inside settled like a stitch under his ribs. Why could he see Stella fitting into their lives like the missing piece of a jig-saw? Was his guilt over Molly, the main thing that had held him back from seriously dating all these years, getting in the way of Charlie's development? Did he need a female figure in his life? Had he prevented Charlie from building a wider circle of relationships with his overprotective fears?

Restricting his own life because he didn't deserve another chance at happiness was one thing, but limiting Charlie's life in any way was the opposite of Aaron's intention.

After dinner, while Aaron loaded the dishwasher in contemplative silence, Stella kept her promise and taught Charlie how to set the timer on his dad's phone.

'Now you can show me how good you are with your numbers,' she said, her fond smile for his son shredding Aaron.

Stella's natural affinity with children and Charlie's awe and trust forced him to admit something he hadn't wanted to explore since the night they'd spent together.

He wanted more than one night.

He probably always had, instinct and the restlessness grumbling away inside telling him this with Stella had never been casual, at least not for him.

But had her desires changed? Perhaps her declaration that she still wanted him in the car had come with the high of successfully delivering the Heath baby. And could he risk exploring this further when Charlie's happiness was at stake?

His feelings might end up putting him in an impossible position: wanting a woman who could disappear at any time and risking that Charlie's feelings might be caught in the crossfire. His son had lost enough.

Charlie let out an excited squeal, alerting Aaron to a change in topic.

'Dad, Dr Stella can ride a horse.' He jumped up on the wooden rocking horse in the corner to show off his skills to their guest. 'Have you got a real horse?' Charlie asked, eyes like saucers. 'I want a pony but Dad will only buy me this one, because it's *dangerless*.' His little shoulders sagged at his dire deprivation.

Stella shot Aaron an apologetic grimace. 'No, I don't have my own horse. They are very expensive and take a lot of looking after,' she said to Charlie. 'I'm just helping other children learn to ride.'

With the dishes done, Aaron needed to usher Charlie upstairs for a bath. Otherwise they could be here all night locked in a plead-denial cycle that they had travelled many times.

'Can you stay a while longer?' he asked Stella after Charlie had reluctantly mumbled goodnight and run upstairs making clip-clop noises. 'I won't be long getting him settled.' She seemed comfortable enough to be here, despite Charlie's energy and constant chatter. And he wanted some alone time with her, to figure out their next move, because his head was scrambled.

'Sure.' She nodded, her smile indulgent despite the lingering reticence in her eyes.

He poured her another glass of wine and took the stairs two at a time. Thirty minutes later, with Charlie bathed, put to bed and a bedtime story read, Aaron came back downstairs to find Stella sitting before the fire. She'd put on an old vinyl from the selection he'd collected over the years, and a pile of Charlie's folded clean laundry sat in the basket on the floor at her feet.

'You didn't need to do that, but thanks.' He grabbed his own wine left over from dinner and took the seat next to her on the sofa.

'Is he asleep?' she asked, tucking her knee underneath her so she faced him.

His head might be all over the place but his body had no hesitations. He took her free hand in his. 'He will be soon. He's exhausted. He didn't even ask for a second story.'

'He's adorable,' she whispered, her face catching the glow from the fire.

Aaron flexed his fingers against hers. 'Did I do the wrong thing by inviting you over?'

She smiled, shook her head, no hint of wariness in her eyes. 'Did I do the wrong thing with the timer on the phone?'

'No. You've made a fan for life.'

'You're obviously very close,' she said.

Was she thinking about her closeness to Angus? Aaron tugged her hand, pressed his lips to her temple and inhaled the scent of her hair.

'We are.' He cleared a sudden blockage in his throat. 'We've had to be.'

Stella's eyes brimmed with compassion and understanding. For the first time ever Aaron contemplated a different reality for his future. Could he try to have a relationship with someone wonderful like Stella? Someone who respected his and Charlie's relationship but also fitted in as if she had always been a vital component?

'I didn't realise that he worries about me quite so much, you know, with the pizza thing and my concerns about the riding,' Aaron said, scrubbing at his jaw as doubts rattled the convictions that had helped him to survive these past five years. How messed up was it that his young son saw through him and his attempts to provide stability. Safety. Aaron was the grown-up; worrying was supposed to be his job.

Perhaps he needed to back off. He didn't want Charlie to grow up neurotic.

'Children can be very perceptive and intuitive.' Stella stroked his arm. 'Don't beat yourself up. If your worst crime as a parent is a bit of burnt pizza, he'll be absolutely fine.'

Aaron took her hand, grateful that she understood his turmoil. 'Clearly Johnny's family set the gold standard when it comes to all things from procreation to perfect pizza.'

Stella chuckled, her fingers making a lazy path on his skin. Was she aware of how her touch inflamed him, held him captive, redefined how he saw himself? Not just as a father, but also as a man.

'You're a great dad,' she said. 'He's just trying to make sense of his world.' That she saw him so clearly was evident in her next statement. 'It doesn't mean he's lacking anything or missing out.'

Aaron looked away, that persistent trickle of shame heating his blood. Of course Charlie lacked a vital part of his life: his mother. And if anyone was at fault, it was Aaron.

'I blame myself,' he said after a pause where Stella gave him the time he needed.

'For the burnt pizza?' she asked, her small, perceptive smile telling him she was kindly offering him an out clause from exposing his deepest doubt if he needed it. Wonderful, caring woman.

'That too.' He laughed, grateful for her attempt at levity, but trusting her enough to want to voice the fear he suspected would haunt him for ever. 'But mainly for Molly.'

Her stare latched to his, unflinching. Holding. Communicating.

I'm listening.

'We hadn't planned to get pregnant with Charlie when we did,' he said. 'One night we ran out of condoms. Molly thought the ovulation maths meant we'd be okay, but I'm a doctor. I should have known better than to risk such an unreliable form of contraception.'

'You wouldn't be the first married couple to dice with the dates.'

He shrugged, futility a hollow space in his chest. 'I guess not, but usually the story has a happy outcome, as ours did for a handful of precious minutes. But a part of me can't help but wonder if things would have been different if I'd been more careful. Protected Molly better.'

'What happened to Molly wasn't your fault.' Her tone was firm. 'You know that she suffered a rare but life-threatening complication of pregnancy that could have happened at any time. It's unfair and tragic and heart-breaking.' She cupped his face, holding his gaze. 'But *not* your fault.'

At his silence she continued, 'Is that why you haven't dated anyone? Because you feel…responsible in some way, because of the timing?'

He shrugged, nodded, sighed, all his ugliness spilling out. 'Every time I look at him I wonder if I'm enough, if I'm doing a good enough job. If I can possibly be everything he needs.'

'You are,' she said without hesitation.

'I'm not so sure. I watched the way he interacted with you tonight. It was lovely to see his confidence.' He frowned. 'I thought I was protecting him—he's lost so much—but perhaps I've denied him a woman's influence in his life.'

'You're doing your best out of love, that's all any of us can do. Life isn't a one-size-fits-all, nor are there any guarantees.'

'That's true.' Stella was so easy to talk to, no doubt that was what made her a great doctor. 'Then sometimes I worry that I'm doing too much, being overprotective, like with the horse riding.'

She shook her head. 'My parents used to worry too. He's the most precious thing in the world to you. It's natural.'

He stared, awed by her calm insights and natural humanity. He couldn't become reliant on her compassion and understanding. He couldn't become reliant on her full stop. He needed to keep emotionally distant for his own sake, too.

Just because he'd glimpsed how well she would fit into their lives if she lived in Abbotsford didn't mean that he and Charlie were what she wanted. She planned to leave as soon as she could, head back to her single life in London. His life, Charlie's life was here, a place from which Stella still felt she needed to run in order to outrun herself, her past, her demons.

And he would wish her every happiness and success.

He and Charlie would be fine, but only if he stayed detached. He owed it to Charlie not to mess up again. That meant maintaining their status quo, their boys' club of two, even if he had to forgo his own needs, which right now urged him to hold her tight…indefinitely.

'I'm teaching tomorrow, at the stables,' she said. 'Why don't you bring him along after my last class for a quick ride? I promise I'll take care of him—I'll have my hands on him at all times. We have riding hats and body protectors. I'll choose our most sedate and docile pony. It will be as safe as possible.'

Her concern and reassurance overwhelmed him. He wanted to kiss her so badly he needed an instant distraction.

The song had changed to a nice, slow ballad.

'Dance with me,' he said, standing.

She frowned at his extended hand. Laughed nervously. 'Really? Here?'

He nodded, recalling a pair of high heels and little black dress fit for a chic, city nightclub.

Soon she would swap her riding boots for dancing shoes and their lives would return to being different.

'You once invited me to go dancing.'

'And you said your clubbing days were over.' She placed her hand in his, eyes alive as she met his challenge.

He pulled her to her feet and into his arms. 'Yes, but there's more than one way to take a pulse.' He caressed her inner wrist over her radial artery and then touched his fingers to her neck where her carotid beat like a drum. 'This is my kind of dance.'

Falling serious because his senses were filled with her scent and warmth, he pressed her close, one hand gripping hers and the other pressed between her shoulder blades. He caught the soft sigh leaving her lips as she looked up at him from under those long lashes.

Fighting the urge to kiss her, Aaron moved them around the space between the fire and the sofa they'd occupied. This was the way he'd held her in the early hours of Saturday morning when he had willed away the first light of dawn, knowing it would bring their intimate time to an end.

She snuggled closer, dropped her head to his shoulder, reminding him how good they'd been together, how their passion had burned out of control until their reservations and differences hadn't seemed to matter.

She'd admitted that she still wanted him. And now that he was touching her again, her heart banging against his ribs and her eyes filled with what looked like longing, Aaron struggled to find the strength to care that he was risking what he valued most: the predictable stability he'd built these past five years.

If only it was just his feelings at risk, he could live with the liability. How could he have what he wanted, more time with Stella, and protect both her and Charlie from growing too attached? His son would be ecstatic at Stella's offer to show him how to ride, but could Aaron allow it, knowing the emotional risks?

Perhaps if it was a one-off…

'I can hear your mind whirring,' she mumbled into his jumper, her hand stroking his chest.

He released the sigh, tugging at the mental knots in his head. 'I want impossible things.'

'What things?' Her finger traced his jaw.

'You.'

She smiled up at him. 'I'm right here, aren't I?'

He nodded, holding her tighter because her presence back in his arms was everything he had craved since their night together. 'I'm trying to protect everyone's feelings…yours, Charlie's.'

She nodded, her gaze softening, growing more

enticing. 'I'm a grown woman. I can protect myself.'

Without waiting for him to process her statement, she reached up on tiptoe, brought her mouth within kissing distance. His lips landed, soft but urgent. She moaned, angled her head, parted her lips to deepen their kiss. He gripped her waist, slid his hands up her back and tangled his fingers in her hair, losing another chunk of his restraint.

She sighed, her whole body collapsing against his chest as if she was exhausted, like him, from fighting this connection that had gone way deeper than either of them expected.

He held her face between his palms and parted from her with a reluctant groan. 'Can you stay the night? Charlie normally sleeps in until seven.' He poured his desires and the unspoken feelings he hadn't yet deciphered into his stare.

How had he gone from content with their one night to being this heavily invested? How would he return to the way he'd been happy with his sexless existence before Stella invaded his world and showed him what was lacking?

Except it wasn't just sex. If he could never sleep with her again he'd still want to see her, to work with her and be on her quiz team. She enriched his existence, and a part of him knew that, if life were different, she would enrich Charlie's too, teach him things that Aaron couldn't.

Her expression shifted through desire to unease. She shook her head. 'I don't want to risk confusing Charlie, but I can stay a while.' She wrapped her arms around his neck, her eyes glazed with passion.

It was a compromise with which he could live.

This time they made it to the privacy of his bedroom, which was at the other end of the landing from Charlie's room, before their passion became overwhelming and undeniable. They stripped in silence, their stares locked, as if both wary, both conscious of what was at stake but unable to fight temptation any longer.

In case this was the last time they would surrender, he commanded every kiss, his passion roaring out of control. He trailed his mouth over her neck, her collarbones, her breasts, every inch of her fragrant skin, learning all of the places that made her fist the sheets and bite her lip to hold in her moans.

Needing more of her, he abandoned her sensitive nipples, pushed her legs wide and covered her with his mouth. Her gasp broke free, her fingers tugging at his hair.

'Aaron.' She whispered his name, a raft of emotions flitting across her expression.

Aaron read every single one. He knew this

woman. He wanted to bring her pleasure, soothe her every hurt, make her promises and never let her down the way she had been in the past.

Dangerous wants.

She shattered, riding out her orgasm with her stare lost in his.

He held her in his arms, kissed her, caressed her until she grew restless and needy once more, wrapping her legs around his hips and clinging to his arms, his shoulders, his back. With protection taken care of, she welcomed him inside her body, her passionate cries smothered by their kisses.

Something cataclysmic was happening. Something he couldn't examine too closely in case it changed his life irrevocably.

Unspoken words clogged Aaron's throat. This couldn't be more than sex, no matter how it felt.

He knew that her internal struggles over their fling matched his. She'd been bitterly betrayed, robbed of her relationship with a little boy she had loved, had spent the intervening nine years protecting herself with only casual dating.

He wasn't ready to forgive himself, to lay all of himself on the line in the search for wholeness, happiness. He had nothing to offer beyond his body and this violent connection they both battled. But a part of him wanted Stella to struggle to forget everything they had shared. As he would.

'Stella.' He gripped her tighter as his body reacted on instinct, driving them hard towards the point of no return. She entwined her fingers with his, matched his every move, alongside him on this journey.

They came together, so in sync it was no use kidding himself that he'd successfully managed to keep emotions at bay.

Exhausted and elated, he dragged her close, burrowed his nose in her hair and fought the temptation to ask her to stay in Abbotsford.

When he woke an hour later the bed beside him was cold. He rummaged for his phone, his heart sinking. He found her text, the screen illuminating the dark room.

I didn't want to wake you. Had a wonderful evening.

He should be relieved that, as promised, she had been considerate of Charlie and so pragmatic that she'd slipped out into the night without disturbing him. There were no loose ends he'd need to explain to a curious five-year-old.

Instead, he was more hollow than he had been in years, as if he'd been robbed of something he hadn't realised he cherished until it was gone.

He threw his phone on the bed, the mess of convoluted feelings inside telling him it was way too late for him to emerge from this unscathed.

CHAPTER TWELVE

STELLA HAD JUST stabled all but one of the Ability Riding ponies when she heard the crunch of gravel that announced a vehicle. Her adrenaline spiked, her stomach fluttering. It was them, Aaron and Charlie.

She tucked some stray hair behind her ear and brushed the hay from her mud-splattered jodhpurs, preening for Aaron, even as she lectured herself to stay impervious. But how could she fight her deepening feelings after last night?

Their passion had moved past sex into uncharted territory for Stella as she'd clung to Aaron and sobbed out her pleasure against his sweat-slicked skin. It had been almost impossible to leave his warm bed and creep out into the night.

Almost. Because of course she'd had to leave.

She had known spending any more time with Charlie and Aaron together was a colossal risk. But she'd done it anyway, because she couldn't fight her need for Aaron any longer. Maybe inviting Charlie to ride had been one stupidity too many.

Sick to her stomach at the fear of falling for Charlie's innocent enthusiasm, wide blue eyes and wicked sense of humour, and also breathless with excitement to see his dad, she rounded the corner of the stables, seeking them out like a kid on Christmas morning.

With every step closer to the car park, she recalled Aaron's heartbreaking vulnerability when he had confessed how he blamed himself for Molly's death. It wasn't that he refused to move on, he was just stuck in limbo by his sense of guilt.

Stella had wanted to hold him and never let him go until she somehow made him believe that he didn't deserve the brutality of his own condemnation.

He was human, that was all. Everyone made mistakes.

But the very reason he had avoided dating all these years, the reason he still only wanted a casual fling—because he couldn't forgive himself—placed him out of her reach. He wasn't ready for a relationship and Stella's own state of mind—she could feel herself slipping deeper and deeper under his spell—was far too prudent to tackle that giant obstacle.

She paused, watched Aaron and Charlie cross the yard, hand in hand, while her stomach churned. It shouldn't matter to her that Aaron believed himself undeserving of a second chance at love, but her careless, weak heart lurched into her throat at the beautiful sight the two of them made. The physiological reaction, tell-tale signs of over-investment—dry mouth, sweaty palms, unable to catch a breath—could mean only one thing: she was perilously close to falling, for all of her caution and good sense.

No, no, no.

What was she doing? She might have been able to recover from dinner with Aaron and Charlie. But sharing his bed, disintegrating in his arms, her every need seemingly answered by the emotions on display in his eyes... It had been too much.

And now her head was full of...terrifying possibilities.

What if she stayed here, in Abbotsford? Could she explore this relationship with Aaron, take time to get to know Charlie, see how it evolved? That sounded like a dream, except she knew from experience that dreams could turn into nightmares. When just the sight of Aaron sent her into a spin, could she stay and risk falling in love with him, with them both?

What if it didn't work out?

They spied her and grinned, waved.

The thought of being that vulnerable, rejected person again made her want to run away. She slapped a smile on her face for the delicious duo. She couldn't let either of them down. Charlie because she had promised him this adventure, and Aaron because she had vowed to take care of his little boy.

'Stella!' Charlie tugged free of his father's handhold and ran the last few paces to her side. 'Can I see the ponies?' He jumped up and down on the spot, his wiry body struggling to contain his rapture.

Stella crouched down to Charlie's level. 'Of course. That's why you're here.'

Time to pull herself together and ignore the feelings she'd stupidly allowed to develop despite all of her warnings. But how could she stay immune to these two men? They'd wormed their way into her heart with their matching blue eyes and identical dimpled smiles and their beautifully close bond. A bond she wanted to protect as much as she needed to armour her own heart.

'But,' she said to Charlie, clearing the clog of emotion from her throat, 'the most important thing about horses, as you will know, because you're a smart lad, is that we mustn't scare them.'

Charlie nodded, his wide eyes at once solemn and attentive.

Stella stood, her gaze meeting Aaron's, and her heart clenched. This was a big step for him, trusting her with his precious son, who was his entire world.

'Hi,' she said, hot and flustered, because the look on his face said, *I'm thinking about what we did last night.*

That was when she felt Charlie's small hand slide into hers. She gripped his fingers, a giant lump in her chest at his trust, his affection almost her undoing.

'How are you?' Aaron asked, his voice low like a secret, distracting her from the tsunami of feelings that almost knocked her from her feet. 'Are you sure you're not too tired for this?'

His implication adding *after our late night.*

Stella yearned to greet him with a kiss, if only to feel lust instead of all the other emotions she couldn't switch off, but she suspected they would still be there, and probably amplified. 'I'm fine.' *On fire, but fine.*

Then she said to Charlie, 'Let's get you a safety hat and body protector. And then we'll meet Zeus.'

Aaron's eyebrows shot up. 'Zeus?'

Stella nodded, her body aching to touch him, to hold him and reassure him that she'd never let anything happen to Charlie.

'Zeus is our most heroic and kind pony,' she

said, as much to Aaron as to Charlie. 'He's special; placid and unshakable. Only very special kids get to ride Zeus.'

She touched Aaron's arm, she couldn't help herself, and shot him an encouraging smile. 'You can sit in the viewing gallery if you want. That's where the parents usually wait and watch.'

Aaron hesitated for a split second, and Stella knew he wanted to be close by in case something happened. 'Have fun.' He ruffled Charlie's hair and backed away, headed for the seating area overlooking the arena. 'I'm going to take lots of pictures so you can show Johnny on Monday.'

Charlie looked up at Stella, awaiting instructions.

Her eyes burned at the trust shown by both of them. At Charlie's innocent excitement and chatter, and Aaron's unspoken belief in her. Tender shoots of hope germinated in her chest. Could she one day be a part of their precious little team? Could she fully commit to a relationship with Aaron, stay here in Abbotsford and give them her all in a way she hadn't done for nine years?

But what if she was once again cast aside, excluded? She'd be back where she was at eighteen: running from her heartache, forced to reinvent herself in order to handle the pain, grieving and alone.

She found Charlie a riding helmet and body protector, ensuring both items fitted correctly.

'Okay,' she said to Charlie, staring into blue eyes so like Aaron's she wanted to hold him too. 'Let's go meet Zeus.'

On Charlie's third lap of the floodlit indoor arena, Aaron's heart settled back into a steady sinus rhythm, each beat forcing him to admit what persisted at the forefront of his mind: his feelings for Stella.

Being with her last night, seeing her with his son, so patient and encouraging, made him admit what was missing from Charlie's life, but more importantly from his own. Yes, he could continue to be everything to his little boy and they would muddle through together, whatever hurdles they faced in life. But he wanted more than that, and perhaps Charlie needed more too.

He wouldn't interfere with her career path, but what if Stella stayed in Abbotsford? They could date, take things as slowly as she needed.

His fingers tightened around the phone in his hand, his heart sore with the sheer volume of emotions coursing through his veins. He'd taken a hundred shots of Charlie riding Zeus, Charlie brushing Zeus, Charlie holding Stella's hand and looking up at both her and Zeus in adoration. But the email waiting in his inbox created a massive distraction to his enjoyment of watching Charlie's dream fulfilled.

Stella's transfer back to a London GP practice had come through an hour ago.

Aaron's first instinct had been to ignore it for a few days, to hide it from Stella and keep her to himself a little bit longer. Because the minute he told her, he would lose her.

But was she his to keep? How did she even feel about him? Would she ever want a proper relationship with dates and sleepovers, shared life occasions and commitment? He understood why she'd wanted to avoid that for nine years, but maybe for her, nothing had changed.

Whereas for him, he no longer recognised himself. He'd try to be okay with casual, but she had destroyed his willpower, bit by bit. Even now, expertly leading the pony by a short rein while walking alongside Charlie, her other hand reassuringly on the back of the saddle, she was still making it impossible for him to resist.

'Dad, I'm doing it, look.' Charlie beamed up at him as he passed the seating for observers on his fourth lap.

'You are awesome,' Aaron said, his gaze tracking to Stella.

Their eyes met. Aaron wanted to leap over the barrier into the arena and kiss her, hold her in his arms and beg her to stay and give them a chance at something real. A new start. A shot at taking their duo and making it a trio.

Try as he might, he couldn't see long-distance working, not with their respective work commitments and Charlie's busy schedule. But there was a growing part of Aaron willing to take the risk, if only Stella felt the same.

As she helped Charlie to dismount correctly, Aaron received a text from Molly's sister, Leah, who had arrived to collect Charlie for his swimming lesson with his cousin, a weekly commitment he and Leah took in turns. Aaron replied and made his way to the stables, his stomach in knots of anticipation.

What if Stella wanted nothing more to do with him and Charlie now that her transfer had been approved? What if she left Abbotsford, left them without a backward glance? On the flip side, could he ask her to give up her city life for a relationship with a single dad tied to a village, who had himself avoided commitment for the past five years?

Charlie was filling the pony's hay net when he arrived.

'Dad,' he said, 'can I take Zeus home? I can brush him and feed him, look.' He held up a handful of hay to prove his utter dedication.

'Zeus does a very important job here,' said Stella, rescuing Aaron from a tricky conversation. 'But, if it's okay with Dad, you can come back and ride him again. Is that a good deal?'

Charlie nodded up at Stella, instantly appeased and worryingly as enchanted with her as Aaron himself. Then he hugged her legs. 'Thanks, Dr Stella.'

She placed her hand on his back, her eyes meeting Aaron's. 'You can call me Stella.'

Bile burned his throat. She had so much power to hurt him, to hurt Charlie, even though the way she swallowed hard, clearly experiencing some strong emotion, gave Aaron hope.

'Aunt Leah is here, Champ.' Aaron hated to break up the moment, but he needed to talk to Stella alone. He should have told her about the transfer straight away. He should have sussed out her intentions for returning to London before he watched her and Charlie bond over a love of horses. Because what if their boys' club of two wasn't enough for her? She would leave and maybe take more than just a piece of Aaron with her.

They walked Charlie back to the car park together. Stella was quiet, but Charlie's horse-related chatter filled the awkward silence.

Aaron only realised he was holding her hand when they approached the car and he saw the shocked expression on Leah's face. Of course, after five years alone, his in-laws, even his own parents would be stunned that he'd met someone with whom he could see a future. He should have anticipated that and spoken to Leah and Molly's parents before inviting his sister-in-law to meet Stella. He'd been just so caught up in his concern for Charlie, so wrapped up in Stella and his awakened feelings, that he'd forgotten there were people in his life who might be momentarily taken aback by the fact that he was ready to move on.

But only before they got to know Stella, witnessed the connection the three of them shared and realised that Charlie was safe in her care.

He turned to Stella as Charlie ran ahead and threw himself at his aunt, who had exited the car to open the rear door, where Charlie's booster seat sat next to his four-year-old cousin's.

'Can you give me a second?' He squeezed her hand. He should speak to Leah before she read too much into the simple gesture. Although a part of him acknowledged that, on his side, Leah's assumptions would be correct. He cared about Stella, deeply.

She cast a quick glance at Leah over his shoulder, a frown appearing and then disappearing just as quickly. 'Of course.' She blushed, pulled her hand free of his and stepped back, putting distance between them.

He reached for her again, his hand on her arm,

because he didn't want her to leave his side. If he didn't have that email on his phone, burning a guilty hole in his pocket, he'd introduce the two women right now, be open and upfront about his feelings.

'Can I give you a ride back to the village? We need to talk.' At her hesitation, he added, 'Please, it's important.'

His emotions rioted in his chest at the doubt he saw in her eyes, the withdrawal that made his stomach churn. Perhaps she wasn't ready to hear that he'd developed feelings for her.

'Sure,' she said, sounding anything but certain. 'I'll...um...just go grab my bag.'

Heartsick, he watched her walk away. Could he ask her to stay in Abbotsford, stay at the practice, stay a part of his life when it meant asking how she felt about him, and—because they were a package deal—about Charlie?

Aaron approached Leah, catching the way her stare naturally followed Stella's path over his shoulder. Aaron turned in time to see Stella, who must have been watching their interaction, dip her head and duck around the corner to the stables.

He quickly asked his sister-in-law if she could wait at his place after taking Charlie to his swimming lesson. He was making a mess of this, but Stella took priority. He would enlighten Leah and the rest of his family about his feelings later, explain that he'd found someone important to him and he'd be exploring a relationship going forward.

If she would have him.

But he was getting dangerously ahead of himself. With Charlie's wellbeing also at stake, he should employ some caution until he knew if Stella shared his feelings. And, as Leah's surprise illustrated, Aaron came with plenty of baggage. He would probably need to reassure Stella that he was ready for a new woman in his life, that she wouldn't be competing with a ghost, that she would be welcome in his extended family too.

He followed in her footsteps, nerves eating away at his certainty. Were his feelings—the happiness he'd finally found, the happiness he had tentatively come to believe he deserved—reciprocated, or had he been kidding himself all this time?

CHAPTER THIRTEEN

STELLA SHOVED HER frigid hands into her coat pockets as she crossed the car park at a brisk pace, just ahead of Aaron. Scalding humiliation eroded a cavity in her chest as the old insecurities of being talked about resurfaced. From the look on Molly's sister's face as she'd walked hand in hand with Aaron, a look of wariness and speculation, Stella would soon be the hot topic of conversation around the village again.

Her heart, which had been bursting with pride for what she now thought of as *her two boys*, had stopped dead for a few terrifying seconds as she came to a chilling realisation.

She wasn't simply filled with pride. She was way too heavily invested in Charlie and Aaron. So invested that she'd actually made a promise to Charlie—to be there any time he wanted to ride Zeus—that she'd never have made three weeks ago.

Had she changed so completely? Committed

herself to staying in Abbotsford? Committed herself to building a relationship with both father and son? But far worse, she had started to imagine dating Aaron, perhaps becoming a part of his life, long-term. His and Charlie's.

That thought, rather than fill her with the warm and fuzzies, sent shivers through her rigid limbs. What a fool.

She climbed into the passenger seat of Aaron's car and stared out across open farmland towards the village as he rounded the vehicle and took the driver's seat. She couldn't work with him, sleep with him, spend time with him and Charlie and not want more. What if it didn't work out? The pain she experienced last time had had long-reaching consequences.

But the way her chest hurt as Aaron and Leah had talked, clearly about her, each looking over at the same moment, told her it was too late for caution. He'd excluded her, perhaps unintentionally, but it had had the same humiliating effect.

She had once again allowed herself too close to a man who didn't share her feelings.

'So…you wanted to talk,' she asked Aaron, keeping her eyes on the road ahead in case he could see the moisture stinging her eyes.

If she looked at him she'd want to beg to be a part of his little tribe. But she wasn't a member. She was superfluous.

She'd sensed the first signs of his withdrawal the minute he'd arrived at the stables today. She'd convinced herself that he was nervous about Charlie's safety. Then Molly's sister had turned up and he'd become even more of a stranger, the explanation falling into place. She was still an outsider and she'd been stupid to allow great sex with a great guy to lure her into feeling something, feeling as if she belonged with them.

From beside her, he reached for her hand. 'Are you okay?'

She nodded too vigorously, avoiding his searching stare and sliding her hand from his to press at her temple. 'I just have a slight headache.' It wasn't a complete lie.

Aaron pressed his lips together and returned both hands to the wheel while Stella recoiled further into herself. This must be worse than she'd thought. He was going to tell her they were done. That it was too confusing for Charlie or too soon for him, or that the family didn't approve.

'Okay, I'll just get straight to the point, then,' he said. 'I received an email today, from the college of GPs.'

Hope wrapped cotton wool around her heart. Maybe he wasn't calling this off. Then it was dashed. Since when had she become so needy? So dependent on him for her happiness?

'Your transfer has been approved,' he continued, his face in profile so that she had no idea how he felt about the news that took her aback. She had almost completely forgotten about the transfer. Become so wrapped up in life here, in the practice, in Aaron.

'There's a place for you at King's Park Medical Centre,' he said, his tone infuriatingly neutral. 'You can start as soon as you want.'

A chill took hold. She wanted to wrap herself in a hug.

It was time to leave, exactly what she had wanted—to return to the safety of her London life, to the risk-free version of herself, to the security of being alone. Glamorous bars, meaningless dates and a continuous source of entertainment.

She should feel elated. She could resume the life she'd planned. She could run away from the gossip that would ensue if the village found out that Stella had set her cap at Abbotsford's beloved single-dad GP. She could run away from her feelings.

So why did she no longer have the slightest clue what she wanted?

'It is still what you want, right?' he asked, glancing at her clasped hands as if he wanted to touch her again.

'Of course.' *No. Yes. I don't know any more.*

Tears throbbed at the backs of Stella's eyes. If

he touched her while she was this confused she might break down. But he didn't move.

She wouldn't cry. She. Would. Not. Cry.

He nodded, his jaw muscles bunched.

Stella looked away to stop herself from over-interpreting his expression as crestfallen. Perhaps he was simply calculating how her absence would affect the practice, reshuffling the clinics to account for the extra patients.

'I can work a week's notice, if you want.' As long as she didn't touch him again or see him outside of work, she could hold it together for one more week. Five working days. Forty long, temptation-filled hours. Couldn't she?

'I don't want to leave you and Toby in the lurch,' she added.

He frowned, as if about to decline her offer. Then he nodded. 'Only if you can, otherwise we'll manage.'

He drove in silence for a few minutes. Then he pulled up outside her parents' house, killed the engine and turned to face her so she was forced to look into his beautiful eyes.

'I'll be honest, Stella. I hoped that you'd want to stay.' The blue of his irises looked cold in the dim light of the car. She couldn't read his feelings beyond disappointment.

'I hoped you'd want to continue this.' He

pointed between them, a frown pinching his eyebrows together.

'Oh?' He meant their physical relationship, their fling, sneaking around, spending a few hours together whenever the urge overcame them and Charlie was asleep.

A lump lodged in her throat, because they had acted together to protect themselves and Charlie by keeping it casual. She should have known better. A big part of her wanted to see more of Aaron, only she'd broken her own rules and fallen in way over her head. Because now she wanted all or nothing. She couldn't be with him and not want to be a bigger part of his life, to share things with him like lazy Sunday morning walks and quiz nights at the pub. Charlie's Nativity play and Christmas morning.

She had found herself again, here with Aaron, or she had realised that she'd never lost herself in the first place, that she could belong anywhere, that it was her decision.

'Aaron… I…'

'I know,' he said, his voice flat. 'I'm a lot to take on.' Frustration gusted from him on a sigh. 'That's why we could take it slow. See what happens.'

She nodded, her heart made of ice. 'That's a lot to think about.'

She didn't want slow. She'd wasted nine years being afraid, holding back, denying herself.

But clearly Aaron needed more time to get over Molly, his grief, his regrets. He wasn't ready to find love again while he believed himself to be undeserving. Could she really stay, put everything on the line once more for a man who might decide that she wasn't what he wanted after all?

If she stayed, she'd want terrifying things, like a relationship. She hadn't had that since Harry and, given her reaction to Aaron's sister-in-law's curiosity or possessiveness—how she'd felt snubbed—she wasn't sure she was strong enough to take the chance again. Not when the stakes were so high, when she was at risk of falling in love with both Aaron and Charlie.

'I get it,' he said, defeat in his eyes. 'It's been fun, right? But it's not enough to keep you here. Those nightclubs are calling. Time to put away your wellies and dust off your dancing shoes.' There was no malice in his tone, only inevitable sadness, the reminder of their differences.

Stella curled her fingers into fists in her pockets. She wanted to deny his conclusion. To say she had changed, or that she'd never been completely content with that life, she'd just been hiding. But what was the point, if that was what he thought of her? That she'd used him while waiting to return to her real life? Perhaps he didn't know her at all. Clearly she had been the one to become over-invested yet again.

But she refused to be that vulnerable this time. She knew who she was and what she wanted and what she was prepared to tolerate. It was time for some honesty.

'You said it yourself, Aaron; you don't really need me at the practice. You never wanted me there. You have your work, the estate, Charlie, your boys' club.'

She recalled the way he'd rushed over to Leah. Had he been reassuring Molly's sister that nothing had changed in his life, in Charlie's? And if Stella was nothing to him, then why would she stay here, just to be hurt down the track?

He scrubbed his hand through his hair. 'You were the one to say there are no guarantees in life. Who knows what's around the corner? You could stick around for a while. We could try to make this work.' A hesitant smile twitched his lips, his stare softening. He cupped her cheek, the warmth of his hand burning her skin. 'Maybe I could fall in love with you, Stella. Maybe you could be a part of our boys' club one day.'

If he'd told her she meant less than nothing to him, she would have been less crushed. She'd heard half-promises before. She had been not quite good enough before. Next time she gave her all to a man, she wanted his all in return.

She dragged in a ragged breath. 'That's exactly the kind of declaration a woman wants to hear,' she muttered, her emotions strung taut like piano wire. Could he even hear himself? Only the part of her that cared more than she should understood that this was a big move for him. Starting something. Opening up his life, his son's life to another woman when his heart was still full of Molly.

But did she want to be the other woman, waiting in the wings while he made up his mind to move on from his wife? She couldn't make all of the sacrifices, hang around like a spare stethoscope while he worked on forgiving himself.

She shuddered away from his touch. 'It's not that easy for me, Aaron.'

Maybe if he had fought a bit harder for her, she might have been persuaded to stay; that was the depth of her feelings for him. But she couldn't be the cast-aside one. Not again.

'Why?' The quashed hope in his eyes knocked the breath from her lungs.

'Because I'd be the one to take all of the risk. Your life is here and it's all plotted out. Your job is here, your entire family. You're even going to inherit the manor one day. You are part of this landscape.' She flung her arms wide. 'Part of local history.'

'I can't help that.' His lips thinned.

'What if I stay and this fizzles out, or worse, fails spectacularly? You have Charlie, but I'd be left with nothing again. I'd have uprooted my life for nothing.'

As she spoke the words she realised how much a part of her wanted to be that brave. To give her whole heart to this wonderful man and his little boy, not for them, but for herself. Because she'd found something in Abbotsford she had thought was gone for ever: she'd found herself, her true self.

Aaron's jaw tightened. 'Of course. Everything you've said is true, and I understand your fears. I guess I stupidly hoped that Charlie and I might come to mean more to you than a risk that's just not worth taking.'

Pain lashed Stella so she wanted to bend double. 'Come on, Aaron, don't pretend that a relationship between us would be easy. You have Charlie to consider. He, quite rightly, needs to be your first priority. But as you said, you also have other people to consider. There's Molly's family for a start. I saw the way your sister-in-law looked at me.'

She'd seen the judgement flicker through Leah's eyes. 'How do you think they'd react to a new woman in Charlie's life?'

Aaron sighed, his body rigid. 'I would hope that they'd continue to support me the way they have since Molly died. But they aren't the issue here. You're just scared to admit that you belong here because of some historical gossip that everyone else has forgotten.'

She dropped her gaze, closed her eyes. 'Stop. We need to stop.'

Now they were simply lashing out at each other. And he was right in part; she was scared. But not all of their issues could be laid at Stella's door.

When she looked up, Aaron's eyes were cloaked in regret, but also defeat. 'I told you we were a mistake,' she whispered. 'Neither of us is ready for a relationship this...complicated.'

But oh, how she'd wanted to be ready. If only he'd given some indication that he was ready to commit to her in return, rather than the vague promise of more one day.

The look he gave her cracked Stella's heart clean in two. He gave a sad shrug. 'Perhaps you're right. I'd better let you go inside, take something for that headache.'

Every step she took away from him as she walked to the front door crushed Stella's soul a little more. Sometimes there simply wasn't a cure, a magic pill. Sometimes you had to simply bear the pain.

CHAPTER FOURTEEN

AT THE END of the following week, Stella tucked her stethoscope into her bag and scooped up the tattered fleece jacket she wore at the stables from the hook on the back of the door. She cast a final look around, checking for any personal belongings she might have left behind, only to find the consulting room at Abbotsford Medical Centre wiped clean of her presence.

Her heart clenched. It was as if she had never been here.

Would she be as easily erased from Aaron's mind? When she left for London in the morning, Stella, by contrast, would carry a giant, gaping hole in her chest.

Now that she was leaving, she finally recognised that she had fallen in love with Aaron. It was all such a big mess—they had barely spoken to each other this week—that she welcomed the space, the physical distance in order to think clearly. Because seeing him every day at work, wanting to touch him, to draw him aside and ask where they had gone so wrong, left her overwhelmed. So she had stayed silent.

Stella was about to switch off the lights and leave when she heard a noise beyond the door and froze. No one else was supposed to be in the building; it was nine pm on a Friday night.

She clutched her phone like a weapon. Medical facilities were always being burgled for drugs, although this was the Cotswolds…

Stella peered through the gap in the door to see Aaron enter from the rear of the practice. His cheeks were aglow with the cold as he shrugged off his coat and placed it over a chair in the waiting room.

Stella's knees weakened with relief and longing.

He looked up and their eyes met.

Confusion moved through his expression. 'You're here—I thought you left earlier.'

Was his voice…hopeful?

Stella nodded, reminding herself not to overinterpret anything where Aaron was concerned. She couldn't be objective. 'I did leave, but I popped back to collect my things.'

Stupid, because she had hardly moved in here at the start of her placement, unpacking the bare minimum so she could make a speedy getaway. Only now it felt as if she was leaving behind a vital piece of herself, but that was less to do with this room and more to do with the man staring at her as if they had reverted to being strangers.

'I just called in to collect something I need for a house call first thing in the morning,' he said in explanation, because awkwardness prevailed in their communications now. 'Then I was on my way round to your parents' to say goodbye.'

Stella winced, wanting to scrub the definitive word from his vocabulary. She wasn't sure she had the strength to articulate a final farewell, not after all that they had been through together.

'Well… I'll…um…get out of your way.' She returned to her consultation room, her senses on high alert as he followed her and filled the doorway.

She paused, willing him to say something that would change the inevitable. A selfish thought, because she had no solution to make things right between them.

'Charlie wrote you a goodbye card,' he said, each word a blow to her stomach. 'He made me promise that I would deliver it.' He held out the envelope with her name written in giant, uneven letters on the front.

She took it, her fingers avoiding his, and slid it into her bag. She couldn't read it until she was back in London. She wouldn't break down in front of Aaron.

'Do you have time to go for a last drink at the pub?' He offered an uncertain smile, some of the old dazzle that had helped intoxicate her flashing in his eyes.

She shook her head, too devastated with longing to speak. Why did she feel as if she were on a ledge above a canyon, about to bungee jump? Suspended in that silent moment before the fall and the screams and the terrifying exhilaration? That moment when you wished you could back up, say you had changed your mind, only it was way too late.

'Right, no.' Aaron nodded with understanding that almost made Stella cave. 'Perhaps we can catch up when I'm next at City Hospital, get a drink then.' The hope in his eyes tore gaping holes through her resistance.

No, she had to be strong, to think of her own needs. When she was ready, she deserved to be loved by a man who was all about her, all in, ready to commit. But nor could she leave Aaron thinking that he had done anything wrong. *She* had been the one to change the rules halfway through the game. She was the one who wanted the impossible, wanted more than he could give.

She loved him. If this was goodbye, she could make it genuine and heartfelt.

She stepped close, cupped his cold cheeks in her palms and held his gaze. 'I had a wonderful time here. Thank you for everything. I'll never forget my time back in Abbotsford.'

Pressure pressed down on her chest so she struggled for air. She'd always remember him and Charlie and how close they'd become in such a short period of time. Only not quite close enough.

'Stella…' He groaned her name, regret stark in his eyes. They glittered with emotions. They spoke to her so clearly that she wanted to stare into them all night until dawn.

'Shh.' She pressed her index finger to his lips. She wasn't strong enough to hear how he wished things had worked out, or how if they had met a year or so in the future the timing might have been better for him.

For an expectant second, his gaze grew intense. Stella's heart thumped. His hands gripped her waist. She thought he intended to push her away. Instead, his stare dipped to her mouth. His fingers clenched. His body became rigid.

Static buzzed in the air, like a storm before the first crack of lightning. She couldn't stop herself. She loved him. Just one last goodbye kiss.

Her finger slid from his mouth, replaced by her lips.

As he had every other time, Aaron commanded their kiss, hauled her body close to his, giving her no room to breathe. Their tongues touched. His fingers fisted her jumper. One hand gripped her neck as if he would never let her break free.

A part of her wanted to be trapped here for ever, physically bewitched with no space for thoughts. But it wasn't enough. Not any more.

To make it last, Stella poured all of the things she was too scared to say, too scared to ask for into kissing Aaron. Their passion escalated more quickly than a dangerously irregular pulse. She wanted him, one last time. Then she would walk away without regret.

As if he'd read her mind, Aaron walked Stella backwards until her thighs hit the desk. She shoved her bag to the floor and perched on the edge, tugging his belt loops to seat his hips between her legs.

Snatching her mouth free of his desperate kisses, she fumbled with his fly. 'Hurry. I want you.'

'Stella…' He trailed kisses down her neck to her clavicle, his hands cupping her buttocks to keep her close.

She shook her head. 'Don't talk.'

She didn't want to hear the question in his tone. She had no answers.

Realising her selfishness, she looked up. 'Do you want to stop?'

He grinned, shook his head. 'Never.' And then

he was kissing her again, reminding her how good they were together, how they could shut out the rest of the world, even their own misgivings, when they touched.

Her mind shut down. All her doubts about leaving and fears if she stayed were squashed by the building compulsion. There was a fumbling free of clothes, his trousers shoved down and her skirt hiked up, and from his pocket he produced a condom.

Out of nowhere, he slowed the frantic pace, kissing her closed eyelids, her neck, the top of her breasts. 'I wish I could take you home, take our time, make it memorable.' His hands caressed her back, pressing them closer, heartbeat to heartbeat.

'Aaron,' she pleaded, because she would never forget one single moment they had shared.

He reared back so their stares locked and all pretence fell away.

She gasped at the vulnerability in his stare. She bit her lip to stop herself from confessing how she felt about him, because for a blissful second she imagined that he felt the same. That he loved her and couldn't spend one second without her, let alone the eighty miles of distance that would be their ongoing reality.

She couldn't trust her intuition. She had been

wrong, so wrong before. Seen what she wanted to see. Believed what she wanted to hear. All she could trust was how he made her feel and that would have to be enough to last her a lifetime.

She pressed her mouth to his, kissed him long and deep as she guided him to her entrance.

Fully seated, he groaned, broke free of her kiss, panted.

'Look at me,' he said as her eyes fluttered shut.

She opened them, enslaved by pleasure.

He cupped her cheek, covering her face with kisses that felt like promises. But she needed certainties.

He unbuttoned her blouse, freed her breasts from her bra and took first one and then the other nipple into his mouth. She moaned, slipping deeper and deeper as he held her with such tenderness and passion combined, her throat ached with unshed tears.

She crossed her ankles at his back. His thrusts took on more determination, and still he held her eye contact, a brand burning into her soul, permanent. Unforgettable.

Stella's orgasm stole her breath, her cries muffled against his chest, against the thudding of his heart, which seemed to say everything that she wanted to hear. Aaron crushed her in his arms as his own climax struck. It seemed that he would hold her for ever as they panted together, coming down from the high.

But she had known it would come to an end.

Aaron withdrew, disposed of the condom and then tugged her close once more, pressing a kiss to her temple and holding her there.

'Stay.' He breathed into her hair. 'I'm falling for you.'

She froze. Suspended. Waiting.

The fine wool of his sweater scratched at her cheek. She was too hot. Or too cold. She couldn't tell.

She just knew that this didn't feel right.

'Don't say that,' she whispered, sliding from the desk and rearranging her clothes.

A tension tightened his swollen mouth 'Why not? It's true.'

'Aaron, please don't.' *It's too late.* 'I'm leaving.'

His stare hardened, a muscle ticking in his jaw. 'That doesn't change how I feel.'

'So you suddenly woke up this morning, my last day in Abbotsford, and realised that maybe one day down the track you might love me, is that it?'

She picked her bag up from the floor rather than look at his hurt expression. He might have strong feelings for her—they were good together physically, mentally in sync, had heaps in common—but that didn't make it love. She'd heard those empty words before. Been manipulated and used by them. She couldn't trust words again, not that he had said those particular three.

'Does it matter when I realised how much I care about you when I never thought I'd care for anyone again?' he asked, frustration in his eyes. 'You don't want to hear it anyway. You're already out of the door.'

Stella shook her head, disbelief and confusion fuelling her flight response and knee-jerk observation. 'The timing feels a little...last-minute.'

Of course he would miss their chemistry after such a long dry spell, as she would. But she'd ruined the sex-only deal with her emotional investment. She couldn't stay, sleep with him over and over and never be certain that her feelings would be reciprocated. She needed to retreat, protect herself. Figure out where she'd gone so spectacularly wrong.

He continued to stare at her. 'You think I would manipulate you to stay with empty words?'

'I don't know.' She was losing her grip on reality. 'I understand, believe me. We have sizzling chemistry. We've just proved that it will be hard to walk away from that.'

She indicated the desk, the keyboard and mouse in disarray.

'But I have to leave. Don't you understand?'

She met his eyes, pleading with him to see her point of view. 'I was the worst version of myself here, Aaron. You brought me home and showed me that I've held on to my associations, my fears for too long. That I'm strong. That I can be strong anywhere. But I've also realised that the next time I fall in love, the next time I give my all to someone, I want all of them in return.'

She didn't add that it was too late for next time; she was already in love like never before.

He scrubbed a hand over his face, clearly confused. 'I'm not him, Stella. We can make this work. I'll be in London once a month for my teaching commitments and you can come home for the weekend. It could work. We could make it work.'

'You're right, you're not him, but it could still fail,' she pointed out. 'You know the cruel twists of life better than anyone. You need more time to heal and forgive yourself. You need to focus on Charlie. You don't need a girlfriend who hasn't had a relationship for nine years and lives miles away.'

His jaw clenched. 'So you're suddenly an expert on my needs, are you?'

Stella swallowed hard, fighting tears, because the one thing she did know was that he didn't love her, he only thought that one day he maybe could.

'No…but I understand my own. I need to think about myself. And I need to get out of here. I'm sorry.'

She made it to the car before the first tear fell.

CHAPTER FIFTEEN

AARON GRIPPED CHARLIE'S hand a little tighter on their walk home from school the following Monday. The weather was as grey and dreary as his mood, but he needed to put on a brave face for his son. He'd had lots of practice this weekend.

'So how was school today?' he asked, trying to distract them both from thoughts of Stella.

'Okay.' Charlie looked up at him with a frown. Was his misery, his heartsickness displayed all over his face? He'd relived their demise a thousand times, each time growing more certain of where he'd gone wrong.

He'd messed up. He'd spent so many years living in the past that when Stella turned his world upside down, it had taken him too long to fully let go of his fear. He loved Stella. He should have told her the moment he realised. Instead he'd tried to protect himself by easing into the confession, sussing out her feelings first, telling himself that she needed to take things slowly.

He clenched his jaw. His regrets were piled so high, he felt caged in, claustrophobic, trapped by his own stupidity. Because after everything she had been through, Stella deserved to know how he felt, even if she didn't love him in return.

'Dad…' Charlie tugged his hand.

'Mmm…'

'Johnny said that he's been to London where Dr Stella is,' continued Charlie, 'and there's a giant wheel that spins you around and around,' he made a washing-machine motion with his free arm, 'and a clock called Big Bell.'

'Big Ben,' Aaron corrected, his stomach sinking. He was never going to get away without some searching questions about Stella's relocation.

Charlie nodded, eyes wide at his father's confirmation that, once again, Johnny was the class know-it-all. 'And the Queen lives there in a gold palace. And guess what, Dad?'

'What's that, Champ?' Aaron's gut twisted into knots.

'The Queen has her own horses, hundreds of them.'

He zoned out of his son's exuberant chatter.

He should never have let Stella go. He should have chased after her sooner. By the time he had called at Stella's parents' house horribly early on Saturday morning, she had already left for London. He'd hoped to convince her that his declaration wasn't a trick to keep her here to ensure a steady supply of great sex. That he loved her. That he should have said it sooner, the minute he had started to feel it, but he'd freaked out, telling himself to go slow, that her caution was natural, expected after she had been so badly hurt in the past.

'Perhaps Stella will be able to ride one of the Queen's horses,' said Charlie. 'She likes riding horses, like me, and she went to my school when she was five. Perhaps if I ever go to London, she could help me to ride one of the Queen's horses too.'

Every mention of Stella's name was like a scalpel between the ribs. 'Maybe, although the Queen's horses have very important jobs to do. They are kind of like soldiers.'

Charlie's eyes rounded at the sheer marvellousness of that concept. 'Can we go and see them, Dad? Can we?' He jumped up and down and then galloped off yelling, 'Giddy up!'

Aaron envied his son's ability to bounce back from unmet expectations. If only he could shrug off his regrets so easily. Stella had been right about him: he had carried guilt for letting Molly and Charlie down, a form of penance for being human. But fear of commitment had gone on long enough. He would always love Molly, but he loved Stella too. And unless he showed her that he was ready to take the chance on them as a couple, a family, Stella, him and Charlie, how could he expect her to take the same risk?

His relationship with Stella had popped holes in his fear as if deflating a balloon. If he was happy, Charlie would be happy. He'd met a wonderful woman who understood his work and his life, and most importantly understood him. They shared the same dreams. Yes, they were both scared, both figuring this thing between them out. But was that reason enough to be apart?

Charlie was swinging on the gate, waiting for his father to catch up, when Aaron arrived.

'Will Dr Stella still help me ride Zeus, Dad? 'Cos I really like her and I really like Zeus.'

Aaron's throat constricted. It was time to do everything in his power to make this work. 'I'm not sure, Champ.'

Here came the question Aaron had been expecting since he told Charlie about Stella's transfer over breakfast. 'Don't you need her at your work any more?'

Yes! Of course he needed her, at work and out of work. It didn't matter where, Stella belonged with them, part of their boys' club.

Aaron hesitated. He always strove to tell Charlie the truth.

'I do need her. I need to tell her that.' And

more. He scooped Charlie up and kissed the top of his head before placing him back on his feet. 'I really like her too.'

'Then you should kiss her, Dad. Johnny says his dad kisses his mum whenever she's mad, and it makes her smile again.'

How could Charlie with his youthful wisdom and uncomplicated vision of the world show him how simple it was to follow your heart?

Aaron's own heart clenched so violently he feared that he might pass out. 'We might need to have Johnny over for tea again some time soon. Clearly I have a lot to learn from that kid. Now, enough about kisses. Let's go and see what Grandma has cooked for dinner, shall we? Because I don't know about you, but I'm starving.'

'I hope it's shepherd's pie. I had shepherd's pie for lunch and it was yum. Johnny says it's made of shepherds but I know that's not right, is it, Dad?'

'No. Johnny's wrong there.' But he certainly had a point about the kissing.

Stella sat in the crowded Southbank bar with Darcy. They'd attended the nearby winter market, and, rather than fill Stella's heart with festive cheer, as it normally would, she only felt frozen to the core.

Stella had arranged to meet her friends for

drinks and dancing in the hope that it would shock her system back to normal. Except every time the door swung open to admit a customer, her stomach swooped with dread. She no more felt like dancing than she felt like taking a plunge in the frigid Thames outside.

To distract herself from the nausea of having made the worst mistake of her life, she looked out at the lights twinkling over the river. Were they dimmer than they had been a month ago?

Everything seemed to have lost its shine.

She wanted to be back in Abbotsford, sitting in the Abbotsford Arms with Aaron in front of the roaring fire. She wanted to wake up on Saturday morning and take Charlie to the stables to see the horses. She wanted to walk across the fields holding the hands of her two boys while they talked about nothing and everything, especially what they would have for dinner.

She had finally opened the letter from Charlie that morning and sobbed her heart out. He'd done a drawing of himself seated majestically on Zeus. The caption read *This was the best day.*

And he was right. In many ways it had been the best day. She had begun to admit her love for Aaron. But it also represented the worst day ever, a day when the rot had set in, destroying all hope.

'You should have stayed,' said Darcy, her gaze sympathetic, despite the bluntness of her message.

'Not this again.' Ever since Stella had returned to the flat they'd shared and she had confessed her dalliance with Aaron, Darcy had been on a mission to point out the glaringly obvious in that way unique to sisters.

Darcy's face crumpled with compassion. 'I know it's terrifying. Believe me, I fought loving Joe with everything in me. But I was just fooling myself.'

'I don't love Aaron.' *Lie.*

Darcy ignored Stella's denial. She knew her too well. 'I understand. It's hard for you after last time. But this is different. Aaron is mature and dependable.'

'He said he was falling for me,' Stella said because she'd drunk two glasses of mulled wine and she had previously omitted that part of the tale.

Darcy's eyes lit up before Stella shook her head.

'You don't believe him,' said Darcy.

Oh, how she wanted to believe him. The need burned inside her like an ember. She shook her head, her cheeks warm with shame. 'I've heard empty words before.'

'And you want actions?' Darcy twirled the stem of her wine glass thoughtfully. 'You want him to prove his love by sky-writing it across the city? Buying you a horse? Moving himself and his son and his practice to London?'

Stella gasped, horrified by the last image. 'No. Of course not.'

The idea of Aaron and Charlie uprooting from Abbotsford was preposterous. Aaron had his job, his family obligations, and Charlie deserved the idyllic childhood both she and Aaron had had growing up in the country. They belonged in Abbotsford.

'So, what did you say?' asked Darcy. 'Did you tell him how *you* feel?'

Stella deflated, crumpling like a paper bag. 'No...' Why hadn't she? She wanted Aaron. She wanted Charlie. She should have told Aaron, fought for him, not run away. What would Charlie think about her broken promise to help him ride Zeus again?

'It sounds to me,' said Darcy, in her eldest sister tone, 'that you were both being cautious, both protecting yourselves.'

'I guess.' Why was everything so clear with a little distance? She didn't want to admit outright that Darcy was correct, but her insides were coiled tight like a spring, desperate to act. Despite all of her talk, Stella had clung to the last shreds of her fear, needing to be certain of Aaron's commitment first.

Neither of them had taken that final leap of faith.

'Of course,' continued Darcy, 'he also has Charlie to think about, so...'

'So I'm going to stop hiding here and tell him how I feel.' She stood, scraping back her stool. 'I belong in Abbotsford with them.'

Darcy grinned. 'That's a relief,' she said, tugging Stella back onto her stool. 'Because Joe has asked me to move in with him, so I'll be moving out too.'

Stella hugged Darcy, her eyes burning. 'I'm so happy for you.'

She just wanted her own happy ending too. She wanted Aaron and Charlie and spaghetti and meatballs.

She pressed a kiss to Darcy's cheek. 'You were right. I do love him. Desperately.'

'Of course you do,' murmured Darcy, squeezing her tight.

Stella laughed, swiping at her damp cheeks. 'Why are you always right?'

Darcy shrugged. 'It's a big-sister thing. Get used to it.'

'I'm leaving now.'

Darcy grabbed her arm. 'You can't drive.'

'I'll take the train.' For her men, she would walk every step back to Abbotsford if she had to, because some risks were worth taking.

CHAPTER SIXTEEN

AARON RAPPED HIS knuckles against the wooden front door, the sting from both the cold and the force of his knock. Impatience pounded at him, so he restlessly paced the front doorstep of Stella's house in London.

She wasn't home.

Frustration choked him until he wanted to punch something. He settled for another attack on the door, although he knew it was futile.

He should have called, but by the time he had fed Charlie and rushed back home for an overnight bag so the boy could stay the night with his grandparents, his desperation levels had reached boiling point. He couldn't live one second longer without Stella in his life, so he'd rushed here to confess. Face to face. Preferably lips to lips and heartbeat to heartbeat. To beg her to listen while he unreservedly poured out his feelings this time, a hundred per cent vulnerable. No more fearful, fumbling *mights*, *shoulds* or *coulds*.

Scrubbing a hand through his hair, he stepped backwards and gazed up at the windows of the house, which were shiny black rectangles of doom, mocking him and his belated declaration.

He dropped his head back in despair and sighed to the heavens. His breath misted in the cold air while he contemplated his next move and where Stella might be at this time of night. The winter chill permeated his clothing. Where he had been overheated from running here from the car, now he shuddered. Perhaps Stella had already moved on. Perhaps she was out on a date right now, trying to forget him and their connection.

He huffed, shaking his head. She could deny it all she liked, but what they had shared was real and exceptional and he planned to tell her that, date or not.

'Aaron?'

He spun to see Stella on the pavement behind him, his heart climbing into his throat.

'What are you doing here?' she said, her cheeks rosy and her beautiful eyes trying to conceal the flare of what looked like, unless he was mistaken, hope. 'Your lecture is next week. Where's Charlie?' She stepped closer, panic making her voice squeak. 'Is everything okay?'

He nodded, struck dumb by relief. Would she

worry if she didn't care? Reciprocal hope surged in his chest like the jolt from a defibrillator.

'He's fine. Everything is fine.' He trailed his eyes over her from head to toe, refamiliarising himself with her outline, her shape, her essence. Had it really only been three days? It felt as if a lifetime had passed since he'd watched her pull away from the practice on Friday night.

'Well, that's a lie actually,' he said, desperate to hold her hands but giving her the space she had said she needed. 'Not everything is fine. I need to talk to you and I'll explain.'

She nodded. 'Come in.'

He followed her up the steps and inside the house—a typical Georgian mid-terrace—his hands twitching to touch her, to pull her into his arms and never let her go again.

They took off their coats and Stella led him into the lounge. 'Have a seat,' she said, her voice high-pitched. With nerves?

He wanted to hold her, to tell her that everything would be okay. Because it would. They'd figure it all out together. But being apart just wasn't an option for him, or for Charlie.

Remembering his son, he pulled the letter from his pocket. 'I brought you this. It's from Charlie. He misses you and wants to know if you have any sway with the Queen or the Horse Guards.' His lips twitched as he handed it over, hoping that Charlie's simplistic view of the world would help Stella to see that nothing was impossible with love on your side.

With his love.

But he was getting ahead of himself.

She looked at the envelope as if it was infectious. At her desperate swallow, her rapid blinking, her choked sob, he snapped and pulled her into his arms. 'Shh,' he soothed. 'It's all going to be okay.'

'I miss him too,' she mumbled into his jumper. Then she laughed, perhaps registering his son's absurd request, finally.

Aaron cupped her cheek and wiped away a tear. 'Stella, I know that you felt you had to leave. I know that you thought I only wanted you to stay for sex. And I know I messed up. I was scared that you wouldn't share my feelings. But I want you to know regardless. I love you.'

He stared into her emotive eyes. Eyes that spoke to him, even in his dreams.

'I'm deeply in love with you.' He cupped her cheeks, swiped the pads of his thumbs over her cheekbones. 'Head over heels and every other cliché you can think of. I was scared to say it in case you could never love me back. In case you didn't want me and Charlie after what you'd been through. But even if I'm not the man for you, even if you won't ever love me back, I want you to know my feelings. Because I want you to move on from your past and be happy.'

'Aaron—'

He pressed his fingers to her lips. 'Please let me finish what I came here to say, what I should have said before you walked away. I'm yours, ready to move on, ready to give you my all. I'll make this relationship work whichever way I can. I'm fully committed to that. To us. You, me and Charlie, who by the way is desperate to see Big Ben. We'll move here permanently if it makes you feel secure about my love.'

She shook her head, tears beading on her eyelashes. 'No... I don't want that.'

Pain sliced him in two. He'd known it was risky to assume that she could love him back, but he didn't regret coming here tonight.

'I see.' He dropped his hands from her face, stepped back.

'Wait.' She lunged for him, wrapped her arms around his neck, buried her face in his jumper and squeezed him tight. 'What I mean is, I don't want you and Charlie to relocate your lives for me.'

Weak with relief that she wasn't kicking him out, that there was still some hope, he pressed a kiss to the top of her head, inhaled the scent of her hair. 'I understand. I'm a package deal. Two for the price of one.'

'I don't care about that either,' she mumbled.

'So are you just wary of falling in love, or specifically wary of loving *me*?'

She surged up and kissed him, interrupting the speech he'd prepared on the drive here after surgery. 'Aaron,' she pulled back to meet his gaze, 'I already love you. And I love Charlie. I missed my boys. I was on my way back to Abbotsford tonight to tell you.'

Everything that he needed to see shone in the depths of her eyes.

'I should have told you before I left, but I was scared.' She swallowed back emotion, breaking his heart. 'Last time love broke me. But I never loved him as much as I love you. Falling in love with you was twice as terrifying. I had so much more to lose if you decided that you didn't want me.'

'You have no idea how much I want you.' He gripped her tighter. 'I wanted you all along. I just had some stuff to work through, because I never thought I'd have a second chance. I never thought I deserved it. But Charlie and I deserve to be happy and whole. And you make us happy and whole.'

'Yes. We belong together.' Her smile glittered with happiness he wanted to put there every day for the rest of their lives.

He crushed her mouth with his, kissed her as

if he'd never have another chance. But he would. He'd take every opportunity to love this woman, to tell her how much he loved her and to show her why he would never stop.

He pulled back, out of breath. 'I want all of you though, not just the incredible sex. I want to hold your hand and sit by the fire folding laundry with you. I want your reminders on my phone—I've made pizza four times since you put that there, just to feel your presence in the house. And when Charlie is asleep, I want to hold you in my arms all night, until you feel as loved as you are.'

She laughed through happy tears.

He tilted up her face and pressed his lips to hers. She tasted like Stella, and salty tears and home. He tangled his fingers in her hair and deepened the kiss, his tongue sliding to meet hers.

'I want you, if you'll have me,' he whispered, his own eyes burning. We'll figure out the geography as long as we're together.'

She cupped his face, pushed her fingers into his hair. 'I want you too. Both of you. And I want to come home, if you'll have me back at the practice.'

'I hoped you'd say that.' He kissed her again and this time they collapsed back onto the sofa so they could do the kissing justice.

'Let's go tonight,' she said when she pulled back for air.

Aaron slid his hand under her jumper, finding the clasp of her bra and popping it open with an expert flick of the wrist. 'The morning is soon enough.'

He pressed a path of kisses down her neck. 'Charlie has a sleepover tonight. I don't want to waste precious hours driving when I could be showing you how much I love you instead.'

'I can't argue with that logic.' She sighed as he divested her of her clothes and found first one nipple and then the other with his lips.

'I must say,' she smiled down at him, her eyes glazed with pleasure, 'this declaration is much better than your previous attempt. Well done.' She gripped his neck and urged his lips back to hers.

All businesslike, he broke free, scooped her up from the sofa and headed for the stairs.

'I've had some coaching from Charlie and Johnny,' he said with a wink. And then he loved her all night long.

EPILOGUE

Three years later

STELLA WATCHED EIGHTEEN-MONTH-OLD Violet chase after eight-year-old Charlie, who had charged ahead waving a stick as if to slay the make-believe dragon inhabiting the woods. Their daughter was never far behind her big brother. She reminded Stella of herself as a child, always chasing a big sister for fear of being left behind or missing out.

But fears of that nature were in the past. She had slain her own personal dragon and joined the boys' club, which had promptly become the Bennett Club, admitting not just one, but two girls to even up the dynamic.

Aaron, walking at her side with a similarly watchful eye on their children, squeezed her hand. 'Are you nervous? About returning to work tomorrow?'

Stella smiled up at her husband, her pulse stirring at the sight of him in a chunky Aran jumper that she wanted to strip off the moment they arrived home from their walk.

Of course, that would be impossible until the kids were asleep.

'A little. I didn't think my maternity leave would last this long.' She shrugged and he wrapped his arm around her shoulders, tucking her underneath so they were as close as humanly possible and still able to walk over the rugged path through the woods.

'Well, I didn't think my parents would want to retire early from running Bennett Manor, so it's all worked out perfectly. You and I get to job share and share the childcare while we enjoy our lives together.'

He glanced ahead to where their children walked hand in hand. Then he dragged her close and kissed her under an oak tree, naked of its leaves but filled with the promise of spring.

Stella lost herself in the glide of lips, the touch of tongues, the wash of love.

Charlie was a caring big brother, always looking out for his baby sister, protecting her and standing up to any perceived injustice, which was sometimes a challenge at bedtime and during their frequent trips to the stables.

A cry split the calm. Stella and Aaron broke apart, their parental senses as alert as their doctoring ones.

'Mum…' Charlie staggered back towards them carrying his sobbing sister.

Stella's heart swelled with pride and love that Aaron and Molly's son was comfortable enough to call her Mum. It had happened naturally and at his instigation, and after the first time Stella had crept off to the bedroom to cry.

'She fell over with this in her hand.' Charlie brandished the pine cone Violet had collected at the start of their walk—they had hundreds of similar specimens at home—and carried all the way, as if it was priceless treasure.

And maybe it was priceless. Because it contained miraculous seeds capable of growing a whole new tree, in the same way that Stella, Aaron and Charlie, with the addition of Violet, had grown their precious little family.

With love.

Aaron scooped Violet into his arms and hugged Charlie with his free arm. Violet snuggled into her father's jumper in a way that Stella envied and adored in equal measure.

'Well done, Charlie.' Stella took the pine cone and accepted a mollified, teary-cheeked Violet from Aaron. She raised her daughter's tiny hand to her mouth and kissed her palm, which bore faint pink indentations from the bumps of the pine cone.

And just like that, Violet smiled, the pain forgotten.

Having received comfort from both her parents, and before Stella could hug her properly, Violet squirmed out of her arms and went to her brother.

Charlie made soothing noises as Violet held up her hand for another kiss. He repeated the gesture and they galloped off together along the path.

Aaron sighed at her side, watching his children scamper away. Stella took his hand as they set off after the pair, her heart full of love for this man who had shown her that being vulnerable was not a weakness.

'What are you thinking?' she asked, knowing the signs of his preoccupation well.

'That I hope all of their trials and tribulations, their hurts and heartaches, are as brief and easily remedied as that.'

'They'll be fine.' Stella smiled, because her husband still worried about his parenting skills. Only now twice as much because there were two humans to love and nurture.

'Yes,' he agreed. Then, 'How can you be sure?'

'Because they'll take after you, and you are infamous around these parts for being a bit of a catch—hot dad doc and lord of the manor rolled into one spectacular package.' She pulled him close for a kiss.

'Maybe they'll take after you—wonderful mother, amazing GP, not to mention your dancing skills.' He twirled her under his arm and bent her back into a dip.

She laughed, her wellies almost slipping from under her in the mud.

'Oh, and I forgot, sexy. You are so sexy.' He wrapped his arm around her waist and hauled her close, this kiss turning X-rated.

'They'll take after us,' she said, holding his hand once more.

Aaron raised her hand to his mouth and kissed her knuckles, his eyes communicating so much love that she grew light-headed. 'I love you,' he said.

'I love you too.'

'I couldn't ask for anything more,' he said.

And then they chased after their children.

* * * * *